Lu

David Huggins was born in London. He is currently working on a new novel about three generations of an acting
family, *Me Me Me*.

Luxury Amnesia

DAVID HUGGINS

faber and faber

First published in 1999
by Faber and Faber Limited
3 Queen Square London WC1N 3AU
This paperback edition published in 2000

Typeset by Faber and Faber Ltd
Printed in England by Mackays of Chatham plc, Chatham, Kent

A CIP record for this book
is available from the British Library

ISBN 0–571–20146–6

2 4 6 8 10 9 7 5 3 1

for Madeleine Christie

Luxury Amnesia

Prologue

Once I was inside the living room the sprung fire-door closed behind me and it was so dark that I couldn't see a thing. I searched for the light switch, wiping the cool wall with my palm. Moving to the left, I realized I'd gone too far, but I knew there was another switch by the kitchen. I thought I could make out the kitchen door so I set off across the room in a chain-gang shuffle, with my arms stretched out before me. Half-way across the room I stopped. Something was wrong and I tensed with cave-dweller alarm. Vestigial body hair pricked up on my arms as I groped for the back of the sofa.

My hand brushed something where nothing was meant to be. Something fleecy. I peered down into the murk and nearly shed my skin.

Someone was sitting there in the darkness.

I ran to where I thought the kitchen door should be and banged into some shelves. A glass vase fell to the floor and shattered. Frantic, I followed the length of the shelf with my hand, reaching out to scrabble for the light switch. I couldn't find it. I was panting and my mouth was dry. I ran my hands over the wall again and again, and then my wrist snagged on the switch and the room lit up and I saw his head poking up over the back of the sofa. I couldn't understand why he'd been sitting alone in the dark. It felt cold, as if a window had been opened.

'Are you OK?'

He made no reply. He sat there slumped, with his head to one side, staring at nothing at all. Blood banged at my temples, trying to squeeze its way out of my head. I stepped over the loose CDs scattered on the floor, knelt down and searched his wrist for a pulse. Nothing. Fear locked my legs. A voice inside told me that it was already too late to call for an ambulance. I stood up feeling dizzy, blinked a few times and gulped some air. There was a look of blank surprise on his face, as if someone had made a joke that he'd got a little late. His eyes looked wrong, lustreless. I tried to tell myself that it was all a practical joke. Then I waved my hand in front of the eyes and I knew he was dead.

I turned aside and vomited, wiped my mouth and forced myself to look at him again. I'd never seen a dead body before. The face was white, thrice-bled. The palms faced upwards and shiny fingers pointed to a brown bottle of sleeping pills that lay on the cushion. It was empty. Had he taken an overdose? Could the pills have killed him that quickly? I'd been gone for twenty minutes, half an hour at most. I felt I ought to close his eyelids but I couldn't bring myself to touch him. I took a cigarette from the pack on the table and lit it, my first in six months. There was a strange clicking sound and I realized that a CD was playing, a notch above the threshold of audibility.

The glass door grated in its aluminium track as I slid it open. When I stepped out on to the balcony the cold night air was filled with the sound of traffic from the main road. Four floors below a car circled the square, its tail-lights matching the glow at the tip of my cigarette. I went back into the flat and stubbed it out. My teeth were dry. Chalk pegs. I looked at his body. Two minutes had gone by and it was hard to believe that he'd ever been alive. The living room went into the black and white of bad dreams. A dying room. A car yelped in the street as somebody squeezed a remote and I sat down in the armchair to try and sort my head out. I even closed my eyes in the hope that things might be different when I opened them.

The entry-phone buzzed.

Realizing that I'd left the front door ajar, I ran to the hall and poked my head out into the deserted corridor, holding my breath as I listened for the squawk of police talk on a radio net.

The buzzer buzzed again, right by my ear. I shrank back in crustacean terror. There was a service entrance at the back of the building and I thought about running, but I told myself to think for once. I closed the door and went back to the living room, opened the glass door eighteen inches and crawled out on to the balcony. Kneeling by the parapet I looked down at the street. There were no flashing blue lights but a big saloon was double-parked directly opposite the building. The sight of it shrink-wrapped my lungs until I could barely breathe. I went back inside, grabbed my coat and headed for the door. If it was the police, they'd be sure to take the lift. My fingers were poised to twist the lozenge of the Yale lock when somebody rapped on the door. Terrorized, I looked out through the fish-eye Judas to see a giant black pupil and a white spinnaker of nose.

The face pulled back and it belonged to Phil Jessup.

1

Phil used to be the singer and I played bass in a band called Overload. Five of us had been together for four years, but the band looked like it wasn't going anywhere, so on my twenty-ninth birthday I decided to chuck it in and look for a proper job. Then the miracle happened: we got signed by a major and our first single became a hit after a few bars were lifted and remixed for use as the soundtrack on a jeans commercial. To everyone's amazement, the song reached number one in the UK and stayed there for six weeks, selling half a million copies in the first week alone. It reached number two in the US. That was three years ago.

We thought we were made for life, but our follow-up single flopped. Overnight, success slunk away. The album was heavily promoted but it died a death and the initial flash-flood of royalty payments from the single dwindled to a negligible dribble. Our next releases went nowhere except in Scandinavia, and Overload eventually shed its third syllable. Having no wish to find myself back in court, I won't describe the exorbitant legal wrangle with our mismanagement company that followed the arrival of our tax bill. After the split, Phil took his bruised and swollen ego to Los Angeles in pursuit of a solo career that had, as far as I knew, eluded him. We'd not parted on the best of terms and had lost touch. If I thought of Phil at all, I imagined him turning ever browner beside a pool, living off a woman, the shadow of a palm tree inching towards him across the water like an accusatory finger.

For me, the last three years had been one long economic snake-slide back to the bottom of the board. I'd ended up signing on and working as a painter and decorator to supplement my dole cheque, and although I'd heard Phil was back in London, he was the last person I expected to see as I made my way to work on a poky starter flat near Farringdon Station at seven o'clock in the morning. The streets were deserted until a gaggle of youngish people emerged from a doorway on the other side of the road. Some came my way and I averted my gaze as we drew level.

'Andy!'

I jumped at the sound of my name and a man pulled away from the group, his face instantly recognizable but unfamiliar, as if I'd caught an unexpected glimpse of my own face in a mirror. Then it was Phil crossing the street towards me, bringing with him memories good and bad. We yelled and slapped backs, checking each other for visible signs of wear and tear. The last couple of years had not been kind to Phil. By the look of things, they'd been downright sadistic. His old leather jacket was making an unhappy transition from worn in to worn out and I asked him how he was doing.

'Good. Why are you up so early?' he croaked.

'Going to work. Decorating a flat.'

He laughed, and despite the hour he seemed more or less sober. Behind Phil's back the pretty people drifted off until only a pear-shaped young man with curly hair remained. He approached us as if he was walking into a cold sea and Phil introduced him as Mark Bowring. His face was puffed and pale from burning his liver at both ends, but when Phil mentioned that I'd played bass in Overload, Mark was delighted.

'Amazing! I saw you at the Town and Country in . . . when was it? I was twenty-three, I think.'

As Mark wrestled with the arithmetic, his eyes crossed, searching for the place where his third eye might be.

'Whenever,' Phil cut in.

'Anyway, you were brilliant!' Mark gushed. 'Fantastic. Let me buy you breakfast!'

His enthusiasm touched me and I couldn't just leave Phil there in the street so we followed Mark as he waddled to The Hope, a pub in Cowcross Street that served the porters from Smithfield Market.

Lit by such plucky rays as could elbow their way through the frosted windows, the bar of The Hope was empty except for a group of night-workers. In the corner a fruit machine played its idiot song for one of them, whose red face pulled back from yellow teeth each time he lost. I was glad that there was no jukebox, because I'd little taste left for new music. Everyone else in the pub had been up all night and I felt out of sorts as it was. At the bar Mark ordered bacon sandwiches, vodka and beer for himself and Phil, coffee for me, and paid for it all without a second thought, a feat I'd been unable to achieve for some years. I offered to contribute but Phil didn't even pretend, so I was sure he was 0-per-cent-financed, the same as me. Mark drank the vodka and his eyes went moist, and as he described his plans to start a band with Phil, I understood that Mark was prepared to pay for studio time. It struck me as sad that Phil had been reduced to sponging off a rich kid. Phil had little shame but even he seemed uneasy about it and tried to change the subject.

'Hey, you know who we saw earlier? Sara Carberry,' he said.

I felt a stab of loss at the sound of her name. Phil smiled and his teeth were new, as white and regular as the keys on a toy piano from K-Mart.

'You know Sara?' Mark asked me.

I nodded, seeing her in our hotel room in Barcelona and in her parents' country house.

'Fantastic,' he said. 'We grew up together in Wiltshire. We were practically neighbours.'

I said that I had to go to work and Mark looked worried, as if the virus of gainful employment might have gone airborne.

'What kind of work?' he asked.

'Painting and decorating,' I said.

His shoulders dropped. It hardly counted.

'My stepmother's always going on about having the dining room redone. You should phone her up.'

'Sure,' I said. 'Why not?'

I wrote down the number and it helped me to push thoughts of Sara aside. Most of my work comes to me by word of mouth and I knew I'd make the call.

'Someone may as well benefit,' Mark sighed. 'He's stealing from me hand over fist.'

I asked him who he was talking about and he blinked at me.

'My father,' he said. 'He's helping himself to my trust fund. That's why he's cut my allowance.'

'Oh, leave it out,' Phil groaned. 'I'm not sitting through all that again!'

Mark's head drooped and his white hands rubbed at his face. It was almost funny. Posh, rich and stupid, Mark had everything to live for, but all he wanted was to get lost in music with Phil. When Mark finally staggered off in search of a taxi, I had little reason to think I'd ever see him again, let alone end up with his dead body on my hands.

I wanted to go to work but Phil persuaded me to stay while he finished his breakfast beer, taking a series of little sips as he complained that another venal management company had sabotaged his career and that a woman had broken his heart in California.

'What heart?' I asked him.

Phil's drive-by libido had often been the most dependable thing about him.

'Oh, come on. You've got me wrong,' he said. 'It nearly killed me, Andy. Nearly killed me.'

Phil's eyes misted, as if tortured by memory. In this case his pain seemed real and I asked him when he'd last seen her.

'Oh, just the other day. She's over here now and I had to have another run-in with her, didn't I? Just so she could twist the knife a little bit more. What about you? Still with Janet?'

'No. No, we're divorced. It's hard to believe we were together for three years. These days I'm lucky if anything lasts three weeks.'

'You call that a problem? I'd call that progress,' Phil said.

'So is Sara still with Dario?'

My heart was thumping so hard I was sure Phil could hear it.

'Dunno,' he said.

Perhaps he didn't.

Sara and I had met on the video shoot for Overload's follow-up single in Spain. She was working as an assistant and we were both going through a bad time with our respective relationships, so we ended up sleeping together and for a moment I thought we were falling in love. We talked it over at the end of the shoot and I agreed to let things lie for a month, but no sooner was I back in London than I had a fight with Janet, caved in and called Sara. This contravention of Tour Rules led to a blissful weekend at her stepfather's house. However, two weeks later Sara told me she couldn't bring herself to leave Dario. Stung and weak, I slunk back to Janet. I had the emotional trajectory of a headless chicken for most of my twenties.

Gargling the last of his beer, Phil was trying to tell me that things were beginning to go really, really well for him. He'd been back in London for two months and was living in Hammersmith, signing on like me, but alarm bells rang in my head when he said that there was a lot of interest in his new songs.

'It's a really stripped-down sound. Very, very exciting . . . just an acoustic guitar. Much more real than anything I've done before.'

I cleaned my glasses with my T-shirt. Specks of cream emulsion paint had lodged in the crevice where the lens met the frame. Phil had a good baritone and just enough charisma to front a band, but he'd never written anything even half-way decent.

'Forget it, Phil. It's over,' I said.

'How can you say that? Look, you've just got to help me with some of the lyrics and then . . . Just give them a listen.'

'No way. I'm through with it. I sold my bass.'

'Your Fender what's-his-face?'

'Stack-knob Fender Jazz. The very same.'

Despite his apparently boundless self-confidence, Phil seemed mortified. He knew how much I'd loved that guitar. When he reached into his jacket, for one appalling moment I thought he was going to pull out a demo cassette, but thankfully his hand reappeared clutching a bag of rolling tobacco. I watched his saffron fingers cocoon the dark strands in cigarette paper, fumbling with his Zippo as he lit it, and I detected a snatched quality to his gestures that hadn't been there before. I'd always envied Phil his poise, and when our nanosecond of fame had come, he'd blossomed in its glare while I'd shrunk back, scared it would find me lacking.

I'd never enjoyed playing live and towards the end I'd begun to suffer panic attacks before going on stage. The backs of my hands would go hot then cold, my thermostat haywire, and my head would feel as if it was going to explode. You need to escape but there's nowhere to go. You open the window and it makes no difference. And then you have to go on stage in front of three thousand kids. When the band split I completely understood why North Ken, the lead guitarist, sought anonymity in a Buddhist retreat. Only Jeff, the keyboard player, flourished, and it was from him that I'd heard of Phil's return from California. Jeff was working as a producer in New York for a couple of months and I was flat-sitting for him in Kilburn while he was away. It was a welcome change from my Anne Frank suite in a Dollis Hill mid-rise, but when I began to describe Jeff's place to Phil, he cut me off.

'I've been there, all right?'

He explained that Jeff had put him up for a few weeks when he first came back to London, but instead of being grateful, Phil was irked by the awful truth that it was not enough for him to have failed – someone else had to succeed as well. Phil had a rash on his wrist that he began to scratch, a flaky pink oval three inches long. Eczema. It was time to go and as soon as we'd exchanged addresses and phone numbers we stepped out into daylight.

If Phil had ever developed a Californian tan, it had long

since disappeared. He looked as if he'd spent the last three years moon-bathing. We walked together along the flank of Smithfield Market, where I left him clocking the posters for new bands that covered a dead shop-front, posters that I'd taught myself to ignore.

As I made my way to work, I hoped I hadn't been too blunt about Phil's musical ambitions, but as an old friend I felt I owed him some honesty. Even if he was still stuck on the hamster wheel getting nowhere but older, I realized I'd missed his company and remembered our single going to number one. Phil and I had celebrated all night with the rest of the band and at eight o'clock the next morning we were heading home in a car laid on by the label when Phil buzzed down the glass partition and asked Mitch, the driver, to stop so he could replenish his money supply at a cash dispenser. We pulled up at a bank and across the road a billboard advertised our album *Luxury Amnesia*. Phil was overjoyed. As the singer, he fronted the group photograph, sucking his cheeks and hooding his eyes. I stood behind him with the others, a tall specky geek with a big nose. Phil took the poster for a good omen and withdrew a hundred pounds, and then another hundred to leave in the machine for whoever happened by. I told him he was crazy, but he insisted that it'd keep us in luck and I was too tired to argue.

Mitch agreed with a seen-it-all shrug, so the three of us sat in the car with the motor running for warmth, watching with red eyes as snow fell on the wet black road. The slats of the billboard revolved, slicing our poster into a packet of Superking cigarettes that turned into a small Japanese blob of a car before a small white-haired lady found Phil's money and put the notes in her pocket. Phil said she reminded him of his grandmother and he jumped out of the car to give her the other hundred. It took all my remaining energy to assure her of his good intentions, but by the time we'd persuaded her to accept the money all of us were really laughing, Mitch included. It had been a moment of real happiness.

2

Emma Bowring sounded surprised when I explained that her stepson had given me her number, but she invited me to stop by her house to give a quote on the dining room. My van was being fixed, so the following afternoon I caught a tube to Great Portland Street. The April weather was making a psychiatric presentation – sunshine one day, blizzard the next, followed by a stretch of cold grey nullity such as the one through which I trudged. The Bowrings' house was in the middle of a long, wide crescent and I climbed the stone steps, pressed the doorbell and waited beneath the dark eye of a small security camera. The door swung open, emitting a blast of centrally heated air that bore an undertone of lavender furniture polish, and then a small woman of sixty appeared before me with her hair in a bun.

'Mrs Bowring?' I said.

The little woman laughed.

'No, no! Mrs Bowring is upstairs. You are the decorator? Come in, please.'

The woman had an accent, German or maybe Eastern European, and I followed her across the tiled hall into a large dining room, where she asked me to wait for Mrs Bowring. I sniffed profit as I costed the job, automatically doubling my daily rate. The walls were covered with expensive blue-and-white hand-blocked willow-pattern wallpaper, and the same pattern was scrunched on the parted curtains of a large sash window that looked on to the street. Above the fireplace hung the portrait of a smug old toff with a gun dog. On the bottom of the gold frame a small plaque read 'Sir Thomas Bowring, 1726–93'. Glad that he'd lived long enough to hear about the French Revolution, I moved on to examine a big oil painting of a stretch-racehorse with a tiny head.

The door opened and I turned round to find an attractive-looking woman of my age observing me. She was wearing a white shirt and her blonde locks were shiny enough to have set a brook bubbling with hair-care effluent all on their own.

'Mrs Bowring?' I said.

'Call me Emma. It's Andy, isn't it?'

I nodded, a bit flummoxed. I'd been expecting someone older.

'So how do you know Mark?' she asked in a posh voice.

The question threw me further off balance. At close range, Emma's gym-figured body reeked of scent, bath oil and aromatherapy – preening aspiring to the status of art.

'Well, I wouldn't say I know him. I've just met him the once, the night before last. He was with some friends of mine.'

She raised an eyebrow.

'Musicians,' I said. 'I used to be a musician.'

'Were you successful?'

'You think I'd be here if I was?'

I was in no mood to dredge up the past. Very occasionally people still recognized me in the street, their eyes widening in wonder before they looked away in something more like embarrassment. Because any thought of the band quickly reduced itself to one essential question: what had caused things to go so spectacularly wrong?

'I wasn't trying to be rude,' Emma said. 'I used to act, you know. That's why I asked.'

'Well, it looks like you did all right out of it,' I said.

'It's my husband's money. I guess it took you and me longer than most to find our true vocations.'

I laughed out loud. So what if she'd married a cheque-book? At least she had a sense of humour about it. The whites of her eyes were unnervingly clear, with the blue-white of total health, like children's eyes.

'You do realize Mark's delusional?' she said.

That knocked the good cheer out of me, and I mentally kissed the job goodbye.

'No,' I said. 'No, I didn't.'

'Still, I'm surprised you dared come here,' she said. 'I'm sure Mark said some pretty dreadful things about us, didn't he?'

Her cool chuckle made it clear that she couldn't have cared less for Mark's opinion.

'Just that you wanted some decorating doing,' I said. 'I guess he deluded me too. Oh well, it was always a long shot.'

'No, no. I do want this room done. The wallpaper! It's like being in a teacup. I'd like it plain and simple. A shade of white.'

If the talk of Mark's mental state had been a strategic preamble to some tough negotiation over my fee, I'd lost the first point, because Emma now knew how badly I needed the work.

'I can provide references if you like,' I said.

'There's no need for that. How much would you charge to repaper and paint the room?'

'Eleven hundred cash excluding materials.'

She locked eyes with me and it felt as if she was reading

my bank balance right off my pupils, the sum displayed in bright-green cash-dispenser numerals.

'You'd do it for eight, but I like you, so we'll make it a thousand.'

We shook on it. The gentle haggling had been a game for her, but I was more than happy with the deal. I reckoned it would take only a week, even working alone – a cushy number. No hassle. We agreed that I'd start in a week's time.

Two weeks later I'd almost finished the job. The Bowrings were spending a few days at Foxton Hall, their country house in Wiltshire, and it was their housekeeper's day off, so I was working in the house on my own, a day or two behind because of a misunderstanding with Emma over the precise shade of Farrow and Ball off-white she'd chosen. Mark's stepmother had turned out to be a little more complicated than she'd first appeared and a little less content, but then the same proved true of most of my clients. Things usually start out well enough (almost like a love affair) but the reality of paintbrushes in the sink, all-day radio and physical proximity soon breaks the spell (almost like a marriage). Then it all deteriorates into an acrimonious dispute over money (almost like a divorce).

That afternoon the doorbell rang and I went into the hall expecting to see the organic-fish delivery man on the small black-and-white CCTV screen, so it was a shock to find Phil shivering out there, looking up at the camera and making a reflex adjustment to his hair. Dots of grey snow blew about him as nature's interference. I opened the door and asked him what was up.

'Come to see you,' he said. 'Mark told me you got the job.'

A police car crawled down the street, its fluorescent lime

and orange go-faster stripe sucking at the scarce light. I pulled Phil inside.

'So they've got the whole place then? Just two of them?' he said.

'The housekeeper lives in a kennel in the basement. They've got another big house in the country too.'

'All right for some,' he muttered. 'Nice bit of architecture. Someone really knew their way around a drawing board.'

I led Phil down the hallway into the dining room and he was determined not to be awed. Together we'd partied in the Sussex rock-broker-belt homes of sordid middle-aged perverts with snooker rooms, antique Wurlitzers and sports car collections. If Phil had ever got his be-ringed and tobacco-stained paws on Emma's place, he'd have splurged on leopard-print wallpaper, trompe-l'oeil murals, Jacuzzis and ropy conceptual art. And as a matter of fact, so would I.

'Not bad,' Phil said. 'You know, I think I could live here, Andy. I really do.'

'Course you could,' I said. 'I could fit my whole flat in the kitchen.'

Phil wanted to look around, so I showed him the library. It was like one of the National Trust houses my mother had dragged me round as a kid, and I imagined her ooh-aahing over the furniture, knowing her place. I turned from this depressing thought to look out at the back garden, where the snow had sugared a pile of dead leaves. I put my hand to the cold glass, wanting to ask Phil about Sara, to pick his brains with a cocktail stick, but I managed to stop myself. She'd chosen to stay with Dario, so why prise open the old wound? Phil threw himself down on a spindly-legged sofa and I told him to get off it because Emma was such a fusser, she'd have screamed if she'd seen him lolling there with his boots rucking the yellow satin cushion. Her husband was even worse.

'The housekeeper told me your friend Mark's due to inherit eight million quid next year,' I said.

Phil just shrugged. I was sure he knew all about it.

'I suppose someone has to,' he replied, picking up a bronze model of a horse.

'Put it back, Phil. They get pissed off if you move their stuff around.'

'OK, OK. I suppose they've nothing else to do, the idle bloody rich.'

'Well, you'd know about the first part.'

'Look, um, I don't suppose there's a chance of any work, is there? I'm skint.'

I agreed to pay him for three hours' 'work'. Phil was a dozy sod, but I knew the half-life hell of no money and I could afford to be generous. Emma Bowring was paying me in cash so as not to interfere with my benefit cheque, and I had a few hundred squirrelled away in a building society account, the fruit of some rigorous budget living. Phil's laziness was a male family trait. It was never clear what his brother did and his shiftless father had drawn unemployment benefit for twenty years before succumbing to heart disease at the age of fifty. The family's needs had been met by Phil's Portuguese-born mother, who ran a cafe in West Norwood.

In contrast to Phil's mustard-and-ketchup-coloured childhood, my own early life in the suburbs had been a black-and-white affair with poor reception, albeit less materially constrained. Dad had spent thirty years with Lloyds Bank, ending up as a branch manager before trading the semi for a retirement flat on the Costa Brava. I'd never fallen out with my parents, even when I dropped out of my Graphic Design course at the University of Medway to pursue a musical career, but I hadn't seen them in the four years since our last family get-together, just before my sister and her husband emigrated to Canada. Mum and Dad had slowly turned into brown wrinkled strangers, bit players from a curious mid-afternoon Australian soap opera.

Back in the dining room discordant piano music jangled on Radio 3, so I promptly retuned to a violin concerto on Classic FM and built a steady rhythm with the Pigeon White: dip, splatter, roll. Dip in the tray, splatter on to the wall and roll the paint around with a faint ripping sound (repeat). Phil helped, but after fifteen minutes he complained of a headache, blaming it on the smell of the paint. I couldn't fan up any real anger. Phil had always been a living refutation of the proposition 'Time is money.'

'This is doing my head in,' he moaned. 'I mean, why bother? You know, in the East white is the colour of ultimate decomposition, like black in the West –'

'You're ranting, Phil. Why don't you make us some tea? The kitchen's through there.'

He left the room and I carried on working, droplets of paint from the roller speckling my forearm. When was Phil going to wake up and smell the coffee, the freeze-dried granules of reality? The access road to the Palace of Wisdom wasn't littered with totalled Lamborghinis, snapped champagne flutes, platinum credit cards and hash-burned tour jackets. From the Bowrings' perspective, framed chartered-accountancy diplomas lined the route and neat bundles of VAT receipts formed the central reservation.

Some time passed before I felt uneasy. I called Phil's name to no effect, so I went to look for him in the kitchen. The kettle had boiled, a squiggle of steam visible against blue mosaic tiles, but there was no sign of him. The bathroom door was shut. I rapped on the hard wood, called his name again and opened the door, only to find the bathroom empty. A cold spot of fear began to revolve on the nape of my neck. Emma had a lot of jewellery – some days each lobe and every other digit sparkled with gold and diamonds – and Phil was broke. I should never have let him into the house. All the doors were kept shut on the upper floors because of the burglar alarm. I ran up the stairs and opened a door on a small gym with a mirrored wall, Narcissus's pool turned through ninety degrees. Closing it, I noticed a door ajar on the second floor.

3

I barged into a big bedroom and saw one of Emma's sweaters draped over the back of a chair. Phil was standing by a chest of drawers with his back to me. He spun round, his face wide with guilt, and I shoved him away from the chest of drawers.

'Fuck you!' I shouted. 'What've you nicked?'

'Nothing. Honest!'

I was furious. The knick-knacks on top of the chest of drawers included a segmented silver fish and a jade carving. I made Phil empty his pockets and a sad little pile began to grow on Emma's dressing table, duplicated in her ormolu mirror. To my surprise, Phil had nothing on him but his personal effects: plastic tobacco pouch, Rizlas, a phonecard, a bunch of keys and half a tube of Fruit Pastilles. His tired-looking wallet contained some banknotes, possibly as much as fifty quid, but I was too incensed to pay this much heed at the time.

'See? I told you,' he said.

'What were you doing up here?'

'Just having a little look around. While the kettle boiled. I can't see – I mean, they're away, so what's the harm?'

I dragged him back downstairs to the dining room.

'You stupid fucker,' I said. 'I'm doing a job here but you didn't give that a second thought, did you?'

He slid down the wall and sat mummifying tobacco

with Rizla paper while I used the roller on the wall.

'You've got this all out of proportion,' he said.

'You got yourself all out of proportion a long time ago.'

'What about you? You call painting other people's houses a job? It's just a slow form of suicide,' he said. 'Mark's all set to finance our new demo.'

'What's with the "our"?'

'You and me. Mark wants to put money into a band.'

'What're you going to call it? The Non-commitments?'

'Come on, Andy! Aren't you sick of living hand-to-mouth?'

'I've had enough of the music business. All the chords have been used up and everybody knows it except for the weenyboppers.'

Phil gaped as the cold words splashed over him. If I was living hand-to-mouth, Phil was living hand-to-eyes and hand-to-ears as well, and I wanted him to know it. But as I watched the fragile hopes gutter in his eyes, I asked myself how deeply buried my own musical aspirations really were. Memories of the day the label dropped us were all too clear for me, the A&R man's words sharp as a paper-cut: 'There's nothing more we can do for you.' I can still see the vertical louvres at his office window (chained together even as the band was being released) admitting a thin northern light that fell on a ficus plant in a white plastic tub full of bark chips. I'd spent the best part of six months in bed after the split, trying to face the truth, crippled with nihilistic despair and panic attacks. Imagine living under water and breathing through a reed. It took me another six months to climb out of the pit in my head and regain something like peace of mind. So what if I'd cut back on my ambitions and opted for the slow track? Not everyone has to set the world on fire. However, there was just enough truth in what Phil had said to grate. I'd just filled a tray with paint and climbed back up the stepladder when the front door opened.

I froze and Richard Bowring's head appeared near the top of the doorway, orange with the winter tan he'd collected in some tax haven along with his dodgy dividends. Jagged lines radiated from his popping thyroid eyes as though he'd been trying to dig them out of his head with a screwdriver.

'Who the devil are you?' Richard barked at Phil.

Phil stayed put on the floor, glaring up across the social divide and a generation. Richard was a control freak, Phil an out-of-control freak, and it looked to me like instant chemical loathing. Richard was in his late fifties, as tall as me, with grey-black hair pomaded back to break in tight little curls above his suit collar. His teeth were gritted as usual and his face had flushed an unhealthy red by the time I jumped down from the ladder.

'Hi there,' I said. 'Don't worry about Phil. He's just here giving me a hand.'

'So I see.'

'Yes, he's just having his tea break,' I said.

Richard fixed me with a reproving look and inspected my paint job with a cold loss adjuster's gaze, pausing to light a small cigar which then dangled from his lips like a slow-burning fuse. I couldn't tell if he'd spent his whole life on the verge of an enormous wobbler or if it was just me. Or the precarious position of a man with a much younger wife.

'You were meant to be finished here yesterday,' he said.

It was a statement of fact but he demanded some sort of answer and I felt myself being drawn into a confrontation with his strong, devious will.

'I'm sorry but I did tell Emma I was running a bit behind. There was a problem with the paint. That's why I brought in some help. To speed things up.'

Richard emitted a little smoke from the twin exhausts of his nostrils and then blew out the rest as a wobbly ring. Nought for effort.

'Well, you should have cleared it first. When do you expect to be done?'

'Probably tomorrow. I'd say definitely the day after.'

'You'd say definitely,' he sneered.

'All things being equal,' I said.

Richard scoffed at the ludicrous proposition.

'Well, why don't you try and surprise me? *Etonnez-moi*, Andrew!'

Richard turned to leave the room and Phil wanked the air behind his back. We heard him climb the stairs and I hoped that he wouldn't find anything amiss up there. A bad-tempered fun-shrinker, Richard was living in a million-pound house but he was quite prepared to haggle with me over the odd twenty, and a tin of paint left in the hall was more than enough to set him off. It was easy to picture him as a redcoat officer in a wig and a tricorn hat losing North America. Emma had told me that he was a property developer, so it was even easier to see him subdividing an old NHS hospital into starter flats.

'What a prick!' Phil said, too loud for comfort. 'Does he think he's better than us or something?'

'Yes, Phil. I think there's every chance he does.'

'Tosser. You can see where Mark gets his problems from, can't you?'

Phil did a little work, applying the final coat to a section of skirting board, and fifteen minutes later we heard Richard coming back down the stairs. I steeled myself for another offensive, but he hurried past the dining-room door, lugging a bulging briefcase. The front door slammed and Phil and I stood at the net curtains as Richard crossed the snow-blown road, moving fast like someone in 1920s footage, to climb into his bright-red sports car.

'What do you call that?' Phil asked. 'The new male menopause?'

I went back to work and Phil sat on the floor chain-smoking while he slapped a little paint on the skirting board. Occasionally he leaned over to tap ash in the general direction of an upturned paint lid with a strike rate of around 50 per cent.

'Isn't this fun?' he beamed. 'I'm thinking of becoming a workaholic.'

Soon after making this pronouncement, he repaired to a pile of dustsheets in the corner of the room for a siesta. Outside the snow turned into rain and I worked long after dark, with water trickling down the black windows. When I called a halt, Phil jacked himself up from the floor with an uncharacteristic bonfire of calories to help me carry some of my stuff out to my van. As I locked the front door he mentioned that he was going to a party in Shoreditch.

'Shoreditch?' I said. 'It's gone wrong, that place. A hotbed of property speculation.'

'The party's at Dean's. Dean Haas.'

Phil had my full attention. Dean had directed the video for our disastrous follow-up single and it was through him that I'd first met Sara. It was no surprise to me that Dean had bought into the Shoreditch property blister, a 'scene' that sounded as spurious as Dean himself. Phil said that he'd been at Dean's place with Mark the night they bumped into me.

'Sara'll be there,' he added. 'Yeah, I saw her with Mark

the other night. She's bust up with her boyfriend.'

I fought to net the billion butterflies that broke free in my chest.

'Why didn't you tell me earlier?'

'I didn't know you were that bothered,' he said.

Dizzy with delight, I floated down the steps and across the road to the van.

4

Later that evening Phil and I made the non-essential car journey to Shoreditch, where, to no one's surprise, Dean lived in a converted warehouse 'space'. As we climbed the concrete stairs, I remembered walking with Sara in the hills above Cadaques while Dean was reshooting some of Phil's close-ups. We'd clambered higher and higher, the location shrinking below us with each step, the air brighter and purer than I'd ever known it . . . But my elation at the news of Sara's break with Dario was cut with a degree of anxiety. What if someone else was already in the frame? I visualized a narrow window of opportunity, a window steamed up by the panting breath of a dozen other suitors. And how often do two people really get back together? Sara would have just turned twenty-nine. What had she ever seen in me? Would she see it again? Had it ever really been there in the first place? The voices in my head grew louder along with the sound of music from Dean's party as I scratched flecks of Pigeon White from my glasses.

'I'm going to need oxygen for the final ascent,' Phil wheezed.

'Try and think of it as free exercise,' I said.

Dean had the whole of the third floor and his front door swung open to the touch, so I followed Phil into an enormous L-shaped living area. Guests hovered in groups and I was sure that some of them recognized us. Phil felt no shame (he probably enjoyed it), but I suffered an acute rush of self-consciousness, almost teenage in its intensity. Three kids were staring and from their matching clothes and haircuts I assumed they were in the same band. Thankfully I couldn't see any musos I recognized, but there was no sign of Sara. Had Phil lied to me just so that I'd give him a lift? Dean was perched on the arm of a sofa at the far end of the living area and as we set off towards him across the electrostatic nap of his carpet someone put on an old trip-hop tune, the sound-track to a bedsit suicide. I didn't belong with these people. It was the wrong place for a meeting with Sara and I was on the point of turning back when Dean spied us and broke away from a Eurasian girl to greet Phil with the stiff man-hug at which New Englishmen excel. Dean's eyes were newly bottled behind a pair of oblong glasses and his brown fringe had been artfully mussed to cover some shot follicles.

'You're looking well,' Dean said to Phil.

'Come off it,' Phil replied. 'I'm thirty-three and I've been playing too long.'

It wasn't even true. Phil was thirty-six, three years older than me, but he'd lied about his age to a tabloid four years ago and now he was trying to believe it himself. We'd all knocked off a year or two when talking to the press. It was about the only thing we'd got right.

Dean remembered me and his slit of fish-mouth widened in welcome, but when we shook hands he flinched from the Van der Graaf snap I'd picked up from his carpet. As the three of us talked small, I discovered that while Dean had been working out, in his eyes at least his career was doing just the opposite. He was getting older in another profession in which youth is at a premium, an overpaid promo director whose dream of a transition to feature films was disappearing fast.

Phil soon got bored and went to dredge the room in search of not so much full as empty penetration with someone he hadn't already fucked. Dean and I watched him introduce himself to a small woman with a stud just below her lipstick line. It looked as if she'd dribbled a drop of mercury out of her mouth.

'I see Phil still can't keep his trousers up,' said Dean, gimlet-eyed with equal parts envy and admiration.

So long as a woman felt warm to the touch, Phil could be counted on to make his tired moves. His standard procedure was to pick out his target's least attractive facial feature and tell her how much he loved it – a truly sickening ploy. Nevertheless, I could have used some of his confidence as I looked about for Sara over Dean's shoulder. Dean boasted about how much money he was making, but I could smell a growing desperation on him, a fear that his was a one-act life and that the audience had already begun to cough and fidget. The new gym-build was a dead giveaway, a rippling V of a torso encased in a V-neck T-shirt to form a directional symbol that pointed inexorably downwards. I felt myself shrink as his talk got smaller still. Prey to the queasy sensation that I was being used as a blank screen on to which he was projecting his latest self-image, I was also aware that if there was only one act in Dean's life, then from where he stood my own span had been cut to a single scene – the sharp isosceles career trajectory of many a DJ, model, pop star and footballer.

With half an ear to Dean's spiel (I recall him speaking of 'film' in the singular), I saw that Phil was now talking to Justin Vernon. Tall, dark and ugly, Justin was Phil's cousin and when the band had taken off Phil had got him a job on the road crew. This wasn't unusual – by the end everyone's girlfriend's brother-in-law was on the payroll in some capacity. I'd never much cared for Justin but at least he'd been free of pretension and I couldn't understand what he was doing with the Easyjet set. When Dean felt my attention wander, he attempted to shore up his credibility by dropping names, truly carpet-bombing the nylon, and I was glad when more people arrived and he scurried off to greet them, back-slapping a newcomer while covertly clocking the rest of the room to see who might in their turn be clocking him.

Searching for Sara, I made my way through the thick and the thin, slipping past a spoilt ex-film-student who had spunked her trust fund on two unwatchable shorts and was still waiting for the call from Hollywood five years on. Mo had been the creative consultant to Dean on our video. The foot of the L comprised an open-plan kitchen area where people were piling paper plates with tacos and enchiladas from a local Mexican restaurant. Most were in the cross-hairs of thirty's zero, either laughing too hard or expending all their energy pretending to be laid-back, their 'casual' clothes and ramshackle hair belying the hours of mirror-time they'd soaked up in over-heated hutches like mine. The narcissism levels were unusually high and I saw two micro-celebrities play the eyes game before going over to massage one another's egos.

I felt a hand on my shoulder and turned to find a short, sharp Scot from a music paper who'd accompanied us on our first headlining tour of Britain until his enthusiasm for the band fell away in predictable correlation to the ticket sales. Topped by a black fright wig, his little big head resembled a white drug-lump and I took a certain pride in the fact that I couldn't remember his name. I shook his tiny hand and his forearm was all sinew, a bundle of plaited pipe-cleaners weighed down by a dollop of black and yellow plastic. Given the size of the man, it was less a watch than a wrist-top computer.

'Andy, man. Brulliant, brulliant,' he said. 'Good to see you. I got someone here who needs to meet you.'

He beckoned to one of the kids with the long hair I'd noticed on my way in. Up close he looked about seventeen.

'Love your stuff,' he mumbled.

'Luke's playing the Academy on Thursday,' said the short, sharp Scot. 'You should come, Andy. It's going to be fanta-astic. I remember when you played there.'

What did he want, a medal? The parasite youth vampire had said hello to me only to impress the kid and I despised him even more when he started telling me about a TV documentary he was thinking of presenting. The kid hid behind his hair, paralysed with shyness, just as I'd been at his age when I'd met an ex-member of Frankie Goes to Hollywood. The short, sharp Scot was the type to pat your back while he pissed on your leg and I felt sorry for the kid, so when he offered me his spliff I took a few tugs on it to be polite.

I wandered into Dean's vast bedroom, snagging my sleeve on a spray of art twigs that zigzagged pointlessly from a big blue vase. A group of people were sitting on and around the Caligula-sized double bed and I saw Phil in conversation with Mark. Mark had washed his hair and it had fluffed up to surround his face like a dark halo, backlit by a rattan lamp. Feeling a lift from the kid's skunk, I said hello to Mark and thanked him for putting me on to the job.

'It's working out really well,' I said.

'Really? Phil says Dad's being appalling,' said Mark.

He had more than the normal ration of public school

charm – enough to make me think that he might really care about my treatment at the hands of his father.

'Oh, he hasn't been that bad,' I said. 'Not compared to some I've known.'

'Come on, Andy. He's been a right tosser,' Phil said.

'And you were charm itself?'

I didn't want Phil to fan up any more trouble with Richard because I was still owed money on the job. Mark held a paper plate so laden with food it had curled over like a giant taco and his other hand clutched a polystyrene cup of red wine. A tannin tide-mark crusted his fat lower lip and he'd spilt wine down the front of his green-and-yellow striped shirt.

'Please, Andy. Don't defend my father for my sake,' Mark said. 'You know he's stealing from my trust fund.'

'I think you mentioned it,' I said.

Mark put down his plate of food and used his freed hand to grip my arm. He looked very like his father, but his eyes flicked away if you looked directly at them whereas his father's almost forced you to look at the floor.

'But it's true,' Mark said. 'I *know*! He lost a fortune on the stock market and now he's desperate!'

He'd nibbled the rim of his beaker and I pulled back as wine slopped over it. Not fast enough. A fair bit splashed over my jeans and trainers.

'I'm so sorry,' Mark said. 'Are you all right?'

There was real anguish in the question. He wanted so much to be liked, maybe because he didn't like himself very much, and I felt some sympathy for him.

'Forget it,' I said. 'It doesn't matter.'

But I looked a real mess, splattered with Pigeon White and now red wine. How would it look to Sara? Mark leaned in close to speak in my ear.

'It really is true, you know. About my father. Every word I said.'

'So just get a lawyer and take him to court,' I told him.

'Of course I would if I had any money! Why do you think he's stopped my allowance? I'm completely broke!'

Phil turned round, dismayed to discover that his golden calf had developed BSE. However, in Mark's case the acronym stood for Badly Spoilt Englishman, because the gold watch on his wrist looked as if it was worth a grand.

'It's just not right,' Phil snorted.

'I know, I know! We have to pay for the studio. How do you like Phil's new stuff?' Mark asked me.

Trapped by his darting gaze, I found myself at a loss for words.

'Really fantastic,' Mark declared.

Phil had never found it hard to take a compliment and he drank it in, thirsty as a scarab on the first day of the rains.

'Oh, Andy, it's amazing we're all going to be working together,' Mark said.

'Now just wait a minute,' I said, itching to cut through Phil's phoney pitch. 'There's no way –'

Sara was standing by the front door.

I weaved my way towards her, glimpsing her eyes, her chestnut hair and the lips I recalled were prone to crack in cold weather. It was a pure joy to see her again. When she saw me we kissed and I tingled at the contact, drinking in every detail of her face, from the vertical groove at the tip of her nose to the dark mark in the iris of her left eye.

'What are you doing here?' I asked. 'Still working with Dean?'

'Oh no, not for eighteen months. I'm back at college. Doing English.'

It was typical of Sara to have turned her life around and I envied her, especially as I'd enjoyed reading books so much as a teenager. For a few months following the break-up of the band I'd even suspected that there was a book inside me. It felt very uncomfortable.

'That's great,' I said.

'It doesn't feel like it! I'm at college all day and I waitress four nights a week. But what about you? Have you got a new band?'

'No, I'm well out of it,' I said. 'I don't even play any more. I'm a painter and decorator.'

'What? Toshing people's houses?'

She seemed amused and it made me feel more than usually inadequate.

'For now. What's so funny about that?'

'Nothing, it's just that I always thought of you as such a muso. It's all you ever talked about.'

'Not any more. I got bored of it. You know, intro, verse, chorus, verse, chorus, middle eight, verse, chorus, fade. There are too many songs already. That's why they just recycle them now.'

'Jesus, Andy. There's loads of good new stuff at the moment. Cheer up, why don't you?'

'Me? I am cheered up! I'm free of it! I just wish everyone could see it's basically all bollocks.'

'So what isn't?'

'I'm still looking,' I said.

Sara shook her head and I hoped I hadn't come across all bitter and twisted. I could tell that she'd already had a few drinks and we went to the kitchen area to get some more. Caucasian Chalk people circled the drinks table, stabbing their pleasure buttons with impunity, thrill-seekers stretching their teens far into adulthood. The elastic was about to snap back in their faces. Sara recognized a pigtailed man I knew slightly, a DJ called Neil Cheston, someone deep into the jungle of his thirties, priming himself for another Holocene night.

'Hi, Neil,' Sara said.

'Sara! Howyerdoing? Great, great,' he replied.

He ducked down to forage for something on the kitchen counter and low-level strip-light told the truth – complexion by Philip Morris, cortex battered by anything that had come to hand in a twenty-year struggle to stave off responsibility. Behind his bogus bonhomie, Neil Cheston was plain terrified, a trowel of ratty jazz beard extruding from his face as tubular anxiety. I followed Sara over to the drinks table.

'Who are all these awful people?' I whispered to her.

'People like you, silly.'

She'd teased me like that in the past and I tried to laugh, telling myself we were re-establishing intimacy.

'Anyway, what brought you here?' she asked.

'Phil. He told me you broke up with Dario,' I said.

She bit her lip.

'I was sorry to hear that,' I added.

'No you weren't.'

There was heat in the way she said it and I flushed thermometer red, the blood pin rising up my neck to fill my face. Sara had seen right through me. People poured into the kitchen and when we'd got our drinks we found ourselves pushed back into the bedroom with the art twigs. Phil and Mark were still conspiring in the corner.

'Phil's on great form, isn't he?' Sara said.

Still mellow from the skunk, I held back an urge to denigrate him. Phil was over Mark like a fly on meat and by that point it was hard to tell which of them was the more deluded.

'Phil's all right,' I said. 'He's trying to get another band together with your friend Mark.'

On the ten-day video shoot Sara and Phil's friendship had weathered a troubled start. Phil had brought one of his girlfriends along on location but he hadn't allowed this to prevent him from making a pass at Sara on the second night. He'd smarted from the chilliness of her rebuff and was visibly shaken when she subsequently had the temerity to share her bed with me, but after three days Phil had been forced to accept this apparent refutation of Darwinian theory. He and Sara had made their peace to wind up as friends – friends who wound each other up. Sara went over to greet them and Mark kissed her hello and then she kissed Phil.

'How you doing, Sara? I nearly didn't recognize you!' Phil said. 'You've put on some weight, haven't you?'

'A bit,' she replied. 'Did I tell you how much I love the new teeth? Do they come out at night?'

'You want to find out?'

Mark put an arm around Sara and they were close and comfortable with each other in a way that only long-term friends can be. Although his little pats and smiles were no more than fraternal, I felt ill at ease because I wanted Sara to myself. Then Mark invited her to a casino on the Edgware Road and to my horror she seemed quite taken with the invitation.

'I thought Mark was meant to be broke,' I said to Phil.

'Well, it's all relative, isn't it?' said Phil. 'Or who you're related to.'

'You've got to come too, Andy,' Mark said. 'I've just found some chips in my pocket.'

'It sounds fun,' said Sara. 'Come on.'

'Sure. Great,' I lied.

5

When Dean saw us leaving he intercepted Sara at the door. Lime-green jealous hatred shot through me when he pulled her aside to whisper in her ear, and I had a nasty intimation that there was something between them. Sara broke away from him and as we all said goodbye, Dean singled me out for a rib-crushing bear hug that left me in no doubt that he remembered my brief affair with her.

'Good to see you, Andy. I mean it,' he said, meaninglessly.

I was pressed to find enough air for a reply from my flattened lungs but it hardly mattered. Sara was leaving with me and it felt like victory.

Down in the street I unlocked the back of the four-wheel fridge so that Mark and Phil would take the seats in there, leaving the front free for Sara, who was trying unsuccessfully to open the passenger door.

'Sorry about that. It's the decentralized locking,' I explained.

The van's exterior was the exact beige of my grandmother's hearing aid and the interior trim might have been inspired by the dark tan of her support hose, but the colours didn't look too bad at night. I opened the door for Sara, hurriedly swiping some rubbish from the passenger seat, only to reveal the gash in its naugahyde cover and a corresponding hernia of foam rubber. Slotted once more into the van's submarine air of rot and chemicals, a scent not allayed by a polychrome forest of Magic Trees suspended from the rear-view mirror, I experienced a further 007 deficit as I twisted the ignition key four times before the carburettor would expectorate a trickle of petrol. Once we were under way, Phil produced a bottle of wine-style drink that he had stolen from Dean's party. He pushed the cork into the neck with a paintbrush handle and under the force of pressure a tablespoonful of wine spurted to the roof, from where it dripped on to my lap.

'Here, Mark,' Phil said. 'Have a drink and tell Andy about your stamp collection.'

I thought I'd misheard him. It was hard to imagine someone like Mark collecting stamps. It was hard to imagine someone like Mark collecting his dry-cleaning.

'Well, it started when I was at school,' Mark said. 'My mother encouraged me and by the time I was fourteen I'd built up a really good collection. Rhodesian double heads, Cape triangles, that sort of thing.'

'Yeah, yeah, but now these stamps are worth a hundred and forty grand, right?' Phil said.

'What?' I asked.

'Oh, minimum,' Mark said. 'Probably quite a bit more.'

Sara looked over at me and we cracked up laughing. Was Mark putting us on about the stamps? I felt close to her again, as if the whole expedition to the casino was a prank and we were just seeing how far we'd take it before we bailed out. In the rear-view I could see Phil hunkered over Mark, attentive as a vulture perched atop a cactus.

'Must be a fuck of a lot of stamps,' I said, recalling the cellophane packets of crap sold by paedophile sweet-shop owners on which certain sad kids at school had blown their pocket money.

'Not really,' Mark said. 'Last year a single stamp sold for

more than a hundred thousand dollars. And Mother always insisted I bought only really good stuff. Actually, the whole collection fits into a folder.'

'And Richard doesn't want you to have it?' prompted Phil.

'Of course not. He's no idea how much the collection's really worth, but he said I'd just sell it and gamble away the money.'

It was six to four on that Richard was right, but I suffered a twinge of paranoia. Had Phil's little expedition upstairs that morning been more purposeful than he'd led me to believe? And now all the talk of a new band. Were they trying to tempt me to steal the stamps for them? Or was it all just a delusion of ganja?

'When did you first tell Phil about these stamps?' I asked Mark.

'Just now. At Dean's,' he said.

I relaxed a little.

'But if they're yours, I can't see why you can't just take them,' I said.

'My father refused to give them to me. He wants to drag me back to Canterbury and Dr bloody Leffler,' said Mark.

'Maybe Andy's got an idea though,' Phil said. 'Maybe I should go round tomorrow and try and get the album for you?'

'Don't be daft,' Sara said. 'Andy'd be accused of theft, wouldn't he?'

'Yes, shut up, Phil. I'm trying to drive,' I said.

'Just hear me out, will you?' Phil whined. 'It wouldn't be stealing. Not if the stamps legally belong to Mark.'

'Well, they certainly don't belong to you, do they?' I said.

Mark pulled out two brightly coloured hundred-pound chips to show to Phil.

'I'm only going to gamble one of them,' he said with a suspect finality.

It was a behaviour pattern I knew all too well from my days in the music business and I was sure Mark would blow the lot. I changed gear, accidentally brushing Sara's jeans with the back of my hand. I apologized and she smiled as we turned off Marylebone Road.

The casino occupied the ground floor of a honeycomb office block, and its name, 'The Mountbatten', was carved into a slab of composite marble. We tunnelled between a pair of bow-tied bouncers into a panelled reception area and when the receptionist saw Mark, his face lit up as if he was being finger-fucked by Camelot's Celestial Hand. As Mark signed us in, the receptionist glanced at me and his little horseshoe smile bent flat the moment he noticed my filthy jeans and trainers. I expected a problem, but Mark was a valued customer and the staff treated him as if he was paying off their mortgages. And privately educating their children.

A bouncer unclipped a braided rope and the four of us passed through a small bar with a tired Raffles theme to enter the gambling hall itself, a windowless room seventy feet long and thirty feet wide, into which an air-conditioning unit was pumping cold, recycled cigarette smoke. Mark and Phil went over to the caisse.

'Let's take a look around,' said Sara.

I nodded, enjoying a Sistine spark of life when she slipped her hand into mine to lead me around the roulette tables while Mark broke his chips. He came over with Phil and tried to press some five-pound chips on Sara and me, saying we could pay him back if we won. I felt awkward about taking his money, but Sara accepted them without a qualm so I took a few myself. Sara and I lost on red while Mark lost four chips betting on his date of birth. The wheel spun again and Mark focused on its whirling and the blurring of the numbers, his big black pupils tracing tiny ellipses as they followed the little white ball. It was the first time he'd looked relaxed since I'd met him.

Mark lost his stake but he smiled as he laid another bet. He lost again and I backed away, afraid that he'd think me the source of his bad luck. For all the speed of the ball, the heavy betters wore the glazed expressions of employees coming off a night shift, and there was a sense of congealed energy to the place. Smokers worked at the fruit machines, paying to play at factory work. Money was wearing fancy dress but it was still as serious as a billionaire at a masked ball. The Mountbatten didn't offer a good night out. Ultimately it offered a good hiding.

Intent on keeping it Up and Light, I reined in my hydroponic negativity as Sara and I moved on to another table. We ran out of chips and when Mark realized this he came over to lavish more on us. He was so happy to give them away that we couldn't refuse. When we'd lost the second batch I wanted to buy some more chips but Sara dragged me off to the bar. I saw Phil and pointed to the exit, but he was mesmerized by the wheel and waved me on, his face a pale triangle in the crowd. Sara and I took a pair of high stools at the bar and I crunched stale complimentary nuts. A decorative ceiling fan revolved slowly above the styled hair of men as Sara ordered us both vodkas with grapefruit juice. I was very close to her, close enough to hear the fabric of her jeans rasp as she crossed her legs, and when she wiped her lips, I wiped my own, wrongly imagining that she was attempting to alert me to the presence of an unwelcome nut fragment.

'It's good to see Mark enjoying himself,' I said.

'I don't know, Andy. It worries me. He says he can only sleep properly when he's lost every penny he can lay his hands on.'

'His problem's not gambling, though. He's got inherited-wealth syndrome.'

'Do I detect a hint of chippiness?'

'No, but I mean . . . Whoever heard of a stamp album worth a hundred and forty grand?'

Sara said that it didn't surprise her at all because Mark had been incredibly spoilt and over-protected as a child. His American mother had stripped Hamleys' shelves clean for him every birthday and Christmas, but had forbidden him to ride a horse for fear he'd crack his skull.

'And he was kept indoors for a whole week after we were caught building tunnels in a haystack,' she added.

As Sara spoke I became aware that I was unconsciously mirroring her posture: legs crossed, elbow propped on the bar, hand on knee. I wanted to find a way to get her away from the others and away from the Mountbatten. I wanted to be alone with her.

'Are you hungry?' I asked. 'We could go for something to eat if you like.'

'I'm OK, thanks. I ate earlier.'

'What was all that with you and Dean when we left? Are you seeing him or something?'

'Or something. When I broke up with Dario. A mistake. It's not important.'

'You should have called me.'

'Maybe,' said Sara.

She got up to go to the bathroom and, knowing I was watching her, put some hip into her walk as she left the bar.

It made me think there was a chance for us and my heart soared on thermals of happiness. A minute later Phil wandered through and bought his own drink for once.

'That's my last bloody tenner. Mark's blown the lot too,' he said, staring gloomily into space. 'You know, he's run up so many debts that he's had to sell his flat?'

We'd both been there ourselves. Phil had been forced to sell his own over-priced dump in Covent Garden and the equity in my flat in Mornington Crescent had been made over to Janet as part of the divorce settlement. Phil sucked his new teeth nervously, as if a bailiff had plans to chip them out of his gums.

'This doctor Mark's been sent to's a wealth therapist,' he said. 'Can you believe it? Seems Mark thinks he doesn't deserve the money. Maybe he should just give it away to a good cause. Like you and me.'

'In your dreams,' I said.

Phil sipped his drink and replaced it on the glass bar-top to make a second wet zero.

'I mean, Mark's a laugh,' he said. 'It's just that there are parts missing. It's a shame we can't get those stamps.'

'Don't even think about it,' I said.

Phil swilled the ice around in his tumbler and stared at it morosely.

'Where's Sara?' he asked.

'In the bathroom. Er, did you know she had a thing with Dean?'

'A shag, as I understand it. No emotional baggage.'

'There's always emotional baggage after twenty-five,' I said, suddenly worried.

'Maybe, but not everyone needs two dozen sherpas to carry it around the way you do.'

Sara was walking over to us and dopamine welled in my

brain at the sight of her. I wanted Phil to scram but he stayed put, so the three of us chatted until Mark came through to the bar, cleaned out. He seemed perfectly content, but there was a feeling of anticlimax in the air.

'I asked to open a line of credit,' Mark said. 'After all, I've paid for the place twice over. But they wouldn't hear of it.'

Sara yawned and I was scared she'd go straight home.

'Listen, Andy,' said Phil. 'Why don't we all go back to yours for a bit? It's right around the corner. What d'you reckon, Sara?'

'If it's not far,' she said. 'And it's OK with Andy.'

'Sure,' I said.

I couldn't cut Phil and Mark loose without appearing crassly predatory, but at least Sara wasn't leaving and I was inwardly jubilant as I drove us all back to Jeff's flat through the industrial light and scarce magic of the Edgware Road.

6

It took us less than ten minutes to reach Jeff's place in Kilburn. His large two-bedroom flat was in a private 1970s block in the corner of a sort of garden square. The block was luxurious compared to my hovel a mile or two up the road in Dollis Hill, and there was even carpet in the hall. The other buildings in the square were old and two of them had been run together to form a tumble-down hotel for transients, toms and no-budget tourists. From Jeff's flat you could see the rubbish strewn across the rotting balconies.

As I parked the van the rain intensified, hosing the square in huge arcs as if the weather god had subcontracted the job to an inept special effects team from Norwegian television. The four of us ran for the building and rode the small lift to the fourth floor, our wet faces colour-separated to red, white and blue blotches by a neon strip above the opaque Perspex ceiling panels. Sara leaned against me and stifled a yawn. When the lift bounced us to a stop, I led the three of them down the corridor and into Jeff's flat. The large living room conformed to the prevailing notion of good taste: a bright suite of furniture was arranged in deference to the wide-screen television; framed posters lined walls that had been painted in different colours; and a freestanding wire-mesh bookcase still bore its barcode tag. There was even a rattan lamp in the corner like the one at Dean's. A sliding glass door gave on to a balcony that faced the square.

'It's a bloody palace, isn't it?' Phil said.

He sounded peevish. I went to join Sara at the window.

'This is a lovely place to live, Andy. You're lucky,' she said.

I was about to tell her I was only flat-sitting when she turned back into the room. Phil was standing in front of the gold record that hung above the music console, a gold record that Jeff had collected for the dance album that had paid for the flat. Phil gawked at the disc and the disc looked back at him, its dark label the pupil of a pinned Goldeneye. It felt like a thousand years since Phil and I had received our gold 45s for 'Waterbed', our singular hit single. My last cheque had been for the not-so-regal sum of £267.15, and that included my publishing royalty for the lyrics. Phil had only his mechanical royalty, so he'd have been lucky if his own cheque had made double figures.

'I like your trainers, Sara. Did you get them here?' Mark asked.

Outside Sara's trainers had glowed in the dark.

'Thanks,' she said. 'I got them in Oxford Street.'

'They're from the future that never happened. Jet-packs and teleportation,' sneered Phil. 'I always thought it was going to be like that, you know. When I was a kid. Unlimited leisure and robots doing the boring stuff. And all we got are the fucking running shoes.'

'You're forgetting about mobile phones,' said Sara.

'It's the brands I hate!' Phil howled, turning up the volume and throwing the knob away. 'That smug tick, the white bloody stripes! And the worst thing's they expect you and me to buy their crap and walk around flashing their bloody logos! And we do it! Can you believe it? We should bill the bastards! Charge them for retina space every time we suffer one of their fucking ads!'

Convinced that Phil's rant had been set off by the sight of Jeff's gold record, I took the opportunity to make the bed and kick my dirty clothes beneath it in the faint hope that Sara might stay the night. When I got back to the living room, I found that Phil had liberated a bottle of vodka from Jeff's freezer, poured shots for himself and Mark, and was now searching Jeff's CD collection for a clue to his success. Leafing through a magazine, Sara was looking bored and I wanted Phil and Mark to leave before she decided she'd had enough. Phil tried to stick on a Robbie Williams CD and I took it out of his hands and put on something better. Mark bolted his vodka and busied himself with the TV remote to comb Ceefax for the result of the mid-week lottery, but even as he tapped directly into the nation's collective will to lose, he bubbled with optimism. Fill a glass with water to the half-way point and Mark was the type to call it half full – if he didn't mistake it for a double vodka and order two more. When he found the winning numbers on the screen, he tried to match them to a heap of crumpled lottery tickets that he'd dug out of his pockets. I had a strong, sickening premonition that he was going to win the jackpot, but fortunately this proved unfounded and he brushed his tickets aside before gulping another shot. His eyes were as black and empty as outer space.

'Well, that's that. I've absolutely no money,' he said.

He leaned back in his chair, none too bothered, but Phil groaned as though this temporary hiccup in Mark's cash flow constituted a moral mushroom cloud.

'Try being a student!' said Sara. 'Why don't you just get

a job for a couple of years? Like everyone else. You might even enjoy it.'

Mark blinked in astonishment.

'Give it a try. You're going to get all that money in the end anyway,' she said.

'What's left of it,' Phil added.

Sara poured herself a shot.

'I've just got to get my stamps!' Mark cried. 'Before Dad sells them himself. I loathe and despise him. And that vulgar, common little bitch he married!'

'Who are you calling common?' snapped Phil.

It was the first time I'd ever heard him display any class solidarity and it surprised me. He'd even voted Tory the only time he had any money. Meanwhile Mark's face had turned crimson.

'I'm sorry,' he said. 'I didn't mean –'

'S'OK, Mark,' said Phil. 'Look, maybe we should ring your father and tell him you've run up some big gambling debts. That you need the stamps to pay them off and that we're holding you till we get paid.'

Phil tried to make it sound as if the idea had just popped into his head, but he'd had too much to drink and I could tell that he'd put in some twisted thinking before making his pitch.

'You can't do that. You'd give the poor man a heart attack,' said Sara.

'More than likely,' I said. 'His housekeeper told me he's got a dodgy ticker.'

'It'd serve him right,' Mark said. 'I wish he was dead and not my mother!'

He stifled a sob and Sara comforted him on the sofa. It was no more than her instinctive response to human suffering, but I felt a pang of jealousy as Mark nestled into her shoulder and began to speak of his dead mother and her long battle with alcoholism and depression. She'd been the heiress to an American dry-cleaning fortune, and every spilt drink, leaking ballpoint and explosive Chicken Kiev in North America (indeed, every shaming incontinence) had been a source of profit. As a child Mark had been taken to see her before bedtime each evening, whereupon she'd read to him from *The Jungle Book* in a soft, slurred voice, six pages at a sitting. Locked in her seamless cocktail hour, his mother had read the same six pages of the book aloud every night for a year. Mark's tale sounded like a polished routine. Sara and Phil laughed, but I found it sad and I said so.

'Oh, Andy, lighten up, will you? You take everything so to heart,' Sara said.

Her remark cut right into me. I wanted Sara's arms round me, or, failing that, a reaction of some kind.

'You know, I think Phil's phone call about some gambling debts is a good idea,' I said to Mark. 'I mean, what could go wrong? If your dad's ripping you off, he's not going to want to tell the police, is he?'

Phil sat forward, cross-legged on the beanbag, lizard-quick and greedy for more. Sara swallowed her surprise. I poured myself a vodka and Phil smiled, raising his glass to me. I hoisted my own, bisecting his eyeball with the brim before knocking it back.

'You can't be serious,' Sara said.

'It's OK. Go on, Andy,' said Phil, barely able to contain himself.

'Well, there are a few problems. I mean, you can't very well ring Richard up and say his son owes you money so you want his stamp collection. How do you know there even is a stamp collection? Richard would realize Mark was behind it and he'd tell you to piss off.'

Phil looked crestfallen.

'So you don't ask for the stamps straight out,' I said. 'You build up to it over a couple of calls, put the pressure on. Make it look as if Mark only mentioned the stamps under duress. And if Richard gives them over, it's not like he's parting with his own money. You make him think he's going to have to shell out, then you show him a way around it and I bet he'll do whatever you want.'

'It'll work, Andy! You're a genius!' said Phil.

'It sounds possible,' said Mark. 'But he hates me so much that he might refuse out of spite. It'd suit him if I was killed. He'd get everything my mother left me.'

'That's rubbish!' Sara said. 'And all this stuff about a gambling debt? Nonsense. The bookie would just sue Mark for the money.'

'No, because the law doesn't recognize a bet as a valid contract,' I said. 'So there's a good chance the marker would be sold on. You know what, Phil? I really think you've got something.'

I went over to the music console, dimmed the lights and put on a generic dance track. Sara came over to me and we danced a bit.

'You were kidding, weren't you? What you were saying,' she said. 'Tell me you were just kidding.'

'Hey, lighten up,' I said. 'You take everything so to heart.'

'God, you're so tricky! I'd forgotten that about you.'

Sara dug a finger hard into my belly and for a second I felt there was a slim chance she'd stay the night. Then Phil found an original *Sketches of Spain* in Jeff's vinyl collection. He didn't really care for jazz but he thought he should, and there was a crack of thunder as the needle hit the record and a hissing downpour of static as the track played in.

After two feet of Miles's trumpet the phone rang. It was the neighbours complaining that we'd woken their baby.

'Yeah well, it's not my fault you had bloody kids, is it?' Phil yelled into the mouthpiece.

I turned the music down and swore at him. I didn't want Jeff thinking I'd used the place for parties. Besides, I felt a bit sorry for the couple. They looked permanently knackered and they never even seemed to go out, except to the shops.

I sat with Sara and laughed as she told me about the made-over boozer where she waitressed in Shoreditch. The bar's walls had been stripped down to bare concrete and the punters sat on tatty 1970s furniture to drink their speciality lager. Passing pensioners peered through the plate-glass windows in blank-faced wonder. Phil and Mark were banging on about contemporary music and showed no intention of leaving. Mark had began to slur and repeat himself, a fat pixie scratching his scalp beneath his bubble of Leo Sayer hair. Around two o'clock he found an OFF button somewhere under there and passed out on the sofa. Sara went to make tea, leaving me alone with Phil in the living room. He rubbed at his eyeballs, burnishing them to a hot dry pink.

'She still really likes you,' he whispered.

'So why don't you fuck off and take Mark with you?' I replied.

'No cab fare. You know, I'm almost tempted to make that call to Richard right now,' he said.

'Don't be daft. You're pissed.'

'We'd only be helping Mark recover his own property.'

'How do you know the stamps are really his? Or that they even exist? You're out of your depth.'

'Now, now. Don't get narked. Nightcap?' he asked, twisting the top off Jeff's bottle of Highland Park.

I declined. Phil took a belt of Scotch the size of Andorra and leaned forward.

'If we get the stamps, we split it two ways. You and me.'

'You're fucked up,' I said. 'You'd better sleep it off in the spare room.'

I wanted them out but that was impossible without a scene, so I just hoped that Phil would soon follow Mark into drunken oblivion. Sara was in the kitchen eating a biscuit and I came up behind her to put my hands on her hips.

'Is Phil still mapping out a life of crime?' she asked, twisting away to steady herself against a cupboard.

'Oh, don't mind him. He leads an active fantasy life.'

'Really? And how about you?'

She wasn't as drunk as Phil but she wasn't sober either.

'I keep thinking, what if you'd been single when we met?' I said. 'What if I kissed you right now?'

'What if I went home?' she replied.

That hurt and I was glad I hadn't asked her to stay the night.

'Oh, don't look so miserable!' she said. 'I like you thinking about that.'

'About what?' I asked.

Had she read my mind?

'About kissing me, silly. But I really ought to go home.'

'If you'll let me take you out for dinner next week, I'll drive you back there now.'

She looked relieved and we took the lift down to the ground floor, close to each other in the cramped space. Printed on the brushed-aluminium control panel, the manufacturer's proposal that the lift could carry a maximum of eight persons constituted a frotteur's charter. My heart was racing and my body felt unwieldy, made of wood and poorly articulated. It was raining outside.

'Where do you live?' I asked her.

'Dalston, but I don't think you should drive,' said Sara. 'I'll get the night bus.'

'That's insane. Why don't you stay here? There's a spare room. I could make up the bed.'

'Well, what the hell?' she muttered.

As soon as we were back inside the lift, she kissed me on the mouth. I felt her hand on the back of my neck, pulling me down. We kept kissing and I wanted her right then and there. I pushed up against her. She resisted for a moment, then she curled a leg round mine and rocked against my thigh, breathing hard. I could feel the heat of her body through her clothes. She tugged my shirt loose and ran her hands across my back. I gasped as she found my erection and began to rub at it through my jeans. I pressed against her to trap her hand until the lift shuddered to a halt at the fourth floor and we floated down the corridor. My hand shook with lust as I struggled to open the door to the flat.

Mark was in the bathroom and Phil was sleeping or pretending to sleep on the beanbag in the recovery position. We tiptoed past him and as soon as we were inside Jeff's bedroom Sara pulled her T-shirt over her head. She turned to face me, shimmying out of her jeans as I tore off my own clothes. She was breathing through her mouth and her eyes were bleary. I pulled her on to the bed and we made love. I slipped out of her, lifted her on top of me and put it back in. Sara swivelled her hips and then she began moving back and forth in a steady sweep, the index finger of her right hand rubbing herself. I slowed until she opened her eyes.

'This is wonderful,' I said. 'I can't believe it.'

She looked at me as if I was mad.

'Light. En. Up. You. Take. Everything. So. To. Heart!' she said through clenched teeth.

I put my hands on her breasts and Sara moaned. Her body was roasting hot. She began to shake before the final snap, pushing herself down hard on to me, and soon after that I pulled out of her to come in midair. We broke apart and lay there panting. I propped myself up on my elbow and stroked her hip. When I tried to focus on a corner of the ceiling, it started to turn, so I looked at the tin Babe Rainbow nailed to Jeff's wall until my head cleared.

'Can we do that again?' I asked her.

'Jesus. Hang on a minute.'

'I don't mean right now. I suppose I meant in a few days.'

'Listen, I like you, Andy. And I know you like me, so you don't need to push it. Just let things happen. It's been a while for me too, you know.'

'You could tell?'

'Yeah, I could tell. And try not to wake me in the morning. I've got the day off from college.'

'Night,' I said.

'Sleep well and don't worry so much. You've got nothing to worry about.'

Feeling better than I'd felt in years, I turned off the bedside light and held Sara as she fell asleep, marvelling at the way her body fitted into my side. It was precision engineering.

'You know,' I whispered, 'I wanted to tell you earlier, this place doesn't really belong to me. I'm just flat-sitting for a friend.'

'So what? Go to sleep.'

7

I overslept the following morning, waking at around ten o'clock with Sara fast asleep beside me. It really had happened and I was tempted to call in sick, but as I reassembled the jigsaw of the previous evening I checked myself, recalling Sara's admonition to 'just let things happen'. I went to the kitchen, rinsed the cleanest mug I could find and used it to drink some instant coffee. On the small kitchen television screen a weatherman stood beside the green mess of the British Isles, pointing to a swirling grey handkerchief of cloud that covered London, enfolding the city and its inhabitants like the wrapping of a schoolboy's unwanted spinach.

Out cold in the living room, Mark and Phil looked as if they were waiting for chalk outlines and body bags. The blue curtains admitted a thin wedge of light shot through with dead smoke and I pulled them back to open the window. Mark lay frozen in an Australian crawl on the sofa with an arm out-flung, one leg trailing on the carpet and his mouth wide open as if to snatch a breath of bad air. His face was slick as pork fat under cellophane and the only discernible sign of life was the bump of his cornea as it zipped about beneath a paper-thin eyelid. Phil lay athwart the beanbag, snoring while a million polystyrene pellets slow-cooked his body. A cummerbund of belly showed between his trousers and his T-shirt.

Two empty wine bottles stood on the coffee table and the sight of them annoyed me because I knew I'd have to replace them before Jeff came back. Worse, the arm of the turntable bumped the needle up against the label of his original New Jazz pressing of *Outward Bound* by Eric Dolphy, on which a tube of cigarette ash now orbited at 33 r.p.m. To my horror, spilt red wine had dried deep into the yellow rug, topped by a question mark of pinkish salt, no more than a token gesture. Livid, I kicked Phil until he grunted. I went to clean my teeth and presently Phil pottered into the doorway, ten green bottles smashed into shards and set in cement on the top of his skull. He'd run some water into a glass and he chugged the liquid down, shuddering as it negotiated his throat. I felt like smashing the glass in his face. But I had a mouthful of toothpaste.

'That's a lot better,' he gasped, trying to convince us both.

'You fucking piece of shit!' I spluttered, foam dripping from my chin. 'Look what you've fucking done in there!'

'What?'

His eyes glittered at me through the spread of his fingers.

'You and Mark. That wine on the carpet! Jeff'll have a fit.'

'What is this?' he said, striving for a boyish innocence he'd cashed in long ago, sitting beside me being interviewed on a daytime television chat show in Birmingham. I was ready to crucify him.

'Get the fuck out of the flat! Right now!'

'Chill out,' he said. 'It's nothing to do with me! Swear.'

'Who's it to do with then?' I asked.

'It was Mark. He couldn't sleep.'

'Your new best friend!' I scoffed. 'Well, you better fix the rug. And replace that bloody wine you nicked. I'm late for work or I swear I'd fucking thump you.'

'But I've got no money,' he said.

'Then get your fat friend to pay.'

I was half-way down the stairs when I realized I'd forgotten the keys to the van. I ran back up to the flat and found Phil on all fours in the hallway going through Mark's rucksack. Phil looked up at me, red-eyed and corrupt, and I swore at him.

'Keep your hair on. I'm just taking a little peek,' he said. 'No harm in it. Mark's out for the count. He gobbled some of Jeff's sleeping pills, didn't he?'

'Fuck it. Take his money. I don't care so long as you get that stuff done like I said.'

I went to get my keys and came back to find Phil still combing through the contents of the rucksack on the blond-wood floor: mobile phone, address book, an empty bottle of ready-made vodka and tonic, a blister pack of tablets and a chequebook from a private bank called, appropriately enough, Child and Co. The wallet contained a gold Amex card and over a hundred pounds in cash.

'Well, well, well. The little fibber,' Phil said.

The pills were Dexedrine, Harley Street diet speed made in Germany. Mark had been using his silver spoon to scoop the remaining grey cells out of his head and I showed the packet to Phil.

'No wonder he couldn't sleep,' he said.

Phil pushed one of the flat white pills out of the packet and dry-swallowed it. I could hardly believe my eyes.

'Have one. It'll sharpen you up,' he said.

'File you to a bloody point, you mean. What's wrong with coffee?'

I saw from Mark's driving licence that he was twenty-eight years old and that he had endorsements for speeding and reckless driving. There was a groan from the living room as Mark embarked on his return to the terror of full consciousness. Phil bundled his belongings back into the rucksack.

'Sort the living room out,' I said. 'And then you both fuck off, all right?'

My mood slowly improved as I drove to Regent's Park beneath a trillion-tog duvet of low cloud. It glowed with a wintry light that threw no shadow, as if Apollo had hit the dimmer switch to save daylight in compliance with some cheerless government directive. The back of the van fumed with tins of paint and heady thinners and I'd built a thunderous headache by the time I pulled into the crescent. Emma Bowring's convertible was parked on a permit-holder's bay and I found a free meter just beyond it. Ildikó, the housekeeper, opened the door to me, a white apron blanking the front of her floral-print dress.

'Morning, Andy. You enjoy a late night?'

'No, no. Tucked up by eleven.'

From her crooked smile I knew I'd failed to fool her. Ildikó was a widow with two grown sons, one of whom had gone back to Budapest to start his own building company. She'd stayed on in London to help Richard bring up Mark following the death of his mother, and one morning over a cup of coffee Ildikó had told me what a lovely sensitive little boy Mark had been.

'Such an angel you've never seen, Andy. Always a smile.'

'Do you see much of him these days?' I asked.

'Not so much, Andy. No.'

She looked sad about it, but maybe it was for the best given the slow-motion catastrophe of Mark's adult life. I only hoped he had enough feelings left to behave himself when he did visit her because it was plain that she loved him as if he was her own son. I went to work on the dining room, wishing I was back in bed with Sara and cursing the job at hand. Cutting into the dining-room cornice along a scaffold plank some six feet off the ground, I projected a giddy future with her. Living together. Kids. I knew that I was supposed to stay in the present and let things happen but I couldn't. It was the first time I'd allowed myself a dream in some time.

The cornice was tiresome to paint, with awkward nooks and crannies that angle-poised my spine. I passed an hour in the bone-headed boredom of childhood car journeys, a fly trapped in a ping-pong ball meditating on nothingness, and at midday I heard Emma come down the stairs and go through to the kitchen to speak with Ildikó. Then she walked into the dining room.

'Good morning, Andy. How's it all going?'

'Never better,' I said.

She was carrying an overcoat and I hoped that it meant she was going out for the day.

'The room looks really superb now,' she said. 'Don't you think?'

'I love it,' I said. 'Sometimes I reckon I was just born to paint it.'

It was impossible to lay it on too thick. Believe me, I'd tried. Emma stood there drinking in her own good taste, a loose fist propping her chin as she pictured the room reproduced in the dot matrix of an interior-design magazine. Mindful of Hitler's daubing, Mussolini's unpublished novel and Tony Blair's college pop group, I've long been of the opinion that interior decoration offers a healthy escape lane for thwarted artistic impulses.

'You are using the Pigeon White?' she asked. 'It looks a little dark to me.'

'Don't worry, that's because it's still drying.'

She pursed her lips. If she was so particular, why hadn't she just hired an over-priced blue-chip decorating firm? She'd known my operation was strictly wood-chip from the start. The only explanation I could come up with was that Emma liked having an ex-musician around, someone else whose creativity had hit a cul-de-sac. Someone with bald tyres on an untaxed van who fed meters beneath the cold gaze of clamper teams and scratched emulsion paint from his watch face in the last spine-chilling seconds before a DSS interview. Someone to reassure her as to the wisdom of the trade-offs she'd made in her own life. Emma dwelt happily enough in appearance's cave – indeed, she had exciting plans to improve the lighting – but underneath she seemed lonely. The winter sun had failed to warm up her marriage. What did she think of when she lay back to let Richard gun his clapped-out heart on top of her? Liechtenstein?

'You must remind me to give you a cheque before you go,' Emma said.

'Oh, right. But, er, I'd prefer cash if that's OK,' I said.

I was trying to make it sound as if the money was of little consequence. The idea's to pretend that you like working for them so much that in a perfect world you'd be happy to paint the house for free.

'Oh, God, that means I'll have to go to the bank!'

She made a pout and frowned, checking a tiny wrist-watch on a thin lizard strap.

'Sorry if it's a pain,' I said.

Emma graced me with a long-suffering blink intended to evoke a string of missed obligations. I pictured lunching ladies snapping breadsticks at an empty seat, burping the gas from a second Perrier. And I pictured Sara alongside me, laughing at Emma's little performance.

'No, no. It's just that I've got to go to the garage,' Emma said. 'Look, I'll see what I can do about your money, 'kay?'

I asked her to pass me the smaller brush from the tray on the table and she looked at me with a hint of rebuke but did my bidding none the less. When she passed the brush up to me, her blouse was undone to the third button and from my vantage point on the plank I saw an arrowhead of white bra below the dark cleft of her bosom. Aware of my awareness, Emma adjusted her tortoiseshell hair-clip and there was mirth in her face when I gulped and turned back to the wall. She had nothing to do but play games. Like her stepson, she was spoilt and bored, desperate for sensation, any sensation. I could almost see her running a gold bath-tap and razoring her wrist, dead-eyed through the steam, just to feel something.

'Thanks,' I said flatly, and daubed some paint on to the cornice.

'You know, Andy, I don't know why but I'll miss having you around.'

Her mobile phone rang in her bag and she jumped as if yanked by some divine cord.

'Hi, darling,' she chirped. 'Yes, I'm on my way. I'm leaving right now. Promise.'

She said goodbye to me as she left the room.

'No, silly,' she said to the caller. 'Nobody. Just a decorator.'

The front door banged shut on her laughter and I went over to the window to watch Emma drive off in her convertible, her face the mask of bitten-down fury customarily affected by the rich women of the area when behind the wheel. As an erstwhile face-puller, Emma had the look off pat.

The phone rang at around two o'clock and I heard Ildikó

pick it up in the kitchen. A minute later she came up the steps into the dining room, breathless.

'Oh, Andy! I don't know what to do! It's Mr Richard's son. The man asks for money!'

'Hang on. Who asks for money?'

'The man on the telephone! He says Mark is in trouble. You must talk to him! Please. I don't understand what he says.'

8

I climbed down the stepladder on crumbling legs as Ildikó's panic crashed over me. My mind fish-tailed in her wake as we made our way to the hall, where the receiver lay unhooked and alive on a semicircular table that stood against the wall. I took a breath and held it in as I picked up the receiver, astounded that Phil had gone and made the call. The handle felt slippery in my grip.

'Hello,' I said.

Ildikó clutched at my sleeve. There was a click on the line and then a flatline burr. Phil had broken the connection and I felt a surge of relief.

'They hung up,' I said.

Ildikó sobbed and I hugged her, feeling the first prickles of guilt in my gut.

'Don't worry,' I said. 'It was probably just someone fooling around. A practical joke. Did he say if he was going to call back?'

'No, but I told him Mrs Emma is coming back soon. Oh, Andy, I'm so scared for Mark!'

I followed Ildikó back to the kitchen, where she switched on the kettle and reached for tea-bags and mugs. Then she stood by the butcher's block, smoothing her apron over and over. I wanted to tell her that it was just Mark and an ex-friend of mine playing games, but there was no way to offer her any reassurance without implicating myself.

'What to do?' she sobbed.

The tea didn't seem to help. She really loved Mark (perhaps she was the only person who ever had) and this made me feel twice as bad. Her face was wet and helpless and I tried to convince her that the call had just been a practical joke.

'What if not? I have to call Mr Richard,' she said.

When I heard that, the blood ran right out of me. To stall her, I suggested that the news might cause Richard needless anxiety.

'It could give him a heart attack,' I said. 'And if it *is* all a practical joke, you'd never forgive yourself.'

Fresh fear bloomed in her face and I felt even worse, but somehow I had to put a lid on things before the Bowrings connected the call to me. I prayed that Phil hadn't been so dim as to make the call from Jeff's telephone. The Bowrings had my number at Jeff's, so if he had and they dialled 1471 I was lost. British Telecom's market research had isolated a demographic of climbing paranoia in their client base and the company had developed a gimmick to make it pay. If you dialled 1471 following an incoming call, a robot voice read you the caller's number. And there was no way I could get to Kilburn, change the phone number, defenestrate Phil and return to Regent's Park in less than an hour. But I had to do something. Telling Ildikó that I was going out for a bar of chocolate, I traded the Bowrings' central heating for the street and found a BT phone booth, its glass wall etched with the split logo-man jumping up and down blowing his own trumpet. I dialled Jeff's number and counted off four digital chirrups before the answering machine clicked in to play me my tremulous outgoing message.

'Phil? It's Andy. Are you there? Pick up the phone!'

Nothing. Next I called the Bowrings' place to block Jeff's

number in case they dialled 1471. It was another involuntary contribution towards Sir Iain Vallance's pension plan. I heard Ildikó's voice say a frightened 'hello' just before I hung up, and felt a new stab of guilt for adding to her woes. Back at the house I found her weeping.

'Oh, Andy! Mr Richard calls to speak to Mrs Emma and I tell him what happens! He's so angry I don't call him, he shouted at me! He is come back here.'

'He's here?' I asked, my mouth drier than a salt flat.

'No, he is coming. To wait for next call.'

I racked my mind for a way to retrieve the situation, ransacking drawers at random. I came up with nothing and went back to work in the dining room, my mind a wasp trapped in an upturned glass, buzzing with bad thoughts. Although I'd only pretended to encourage Phil in his fool plan so as to provoke Sara, it was partly my fault and the guilt was exacerbated by the strength of Ildikó's feelings for Mark. Half an hour passed before Emma returned home, and I braced myself for an interrogation. Deny everything. Admit nothing. She went through to the kitchen to confer with Ildikó and then she came into the dining room, sucking on a Silk Cut as if she wanted to get rid of it.

'What happened, Andy? What did he say?'

'Who?'

'The man who called!'

I chose my words carefully and tried to act dumb, which shouldn't have been as hard as it was.

'Ildikó just asked me to talk to some bloke,' I said. 'I picked up the phone but the line was dead. I'm afraid that's it.'

'That's it? This is serious. You know Mark's unbalanced. He's meant to be in a clinic in Canterbury and his father's worried sick about him.'

'Like I told you, I don't really know Mark,' I said.

Emma sighed as if she was letting it go and I entertained a short-lived glimmer of hope that I was in the clear.

'Ildikó says you told her this is all some practical joke,' she said.

My heart did a back-flip and Emma seemed to scour my face for a trace of involvement. I busied myself with the roller to cover my consternation.

'I only said that to calm her down. She was pretty upset.'

Then the phone rang.

Emma went to take the call and I followed her into the hall, dread bubbling up from my stomach into my brain. She picked up the receiver.

'Hello?' she said. 'Who is this?'

Emma flinched at something and I saw her face go white in the mirror before she shooed me back into the dining room. A demented piano piece was blaring on Radio 3, so I couldn't hear Emma's end of the call. When she came back into the dining room she looked stricken and I tried to act calm.

'Was that them? What did they say?' I asked.

'Some man wanted to speak to Richard. He says Mark owes him money.'

She spoke the words mechanically. The call had shocked her and I guessed that the reality of Mark's plight was finally sinking in.

'Turn the radio off, would you?' she said. 'I can't hear myself think.'

I did as she asked and Emma went over to the window to look out at the street, as if she was searching for an answer in the configuration of the parked cars. There was a growling noise outside and then Richard pulled up in his sports car, the carburettors spritzing a fiver's worth of petrol into the engine as he backed into a permit-holder's bay. The front door opened and then it slammed shut.

'Emma? Where are you?' Richard boomed.

The enormous house gave him an excuse to do a lot of yelling. It was no doubt one of the reasons he chose to live there.

'I'm in here!' she called back.

Richard came into the dining room, his face flushed beneath his tan.

'What's happening?' he asked.

He ignored me entirely, or, more precisely, he didn't see me any more than he'd have seen a cube-faced offender on television. I didn't exist for him, in the same way that rich people automatically airbrush the homeless from the streets. I knew that I'd done the same thing when I'd had a lot of money.

'The man called back,' Emma said. 'He said Mark owes him eight thousand pounds. Over some gambling debt.'

'And Mark? Is he all right?' Richard asked.

Beneath the bluster I thought I could detect a note of fear in his voice, something I hadn't heard before.

'They wouldn't let me speak to him,' Emma said. 'Oh, God, the man said if we tell the police he'll kill Mark! I think he meant it. And he sounded Jamaican. It's not surprising Ildikó couldn't understand him.'

Despite everything I almost cracked up laughing. It was hard to believe that Emma had fallen for Phil's dreadful Jamaican accent. His attempt at toasting on one of *Luxury Amnesia*'s filler tracks had been a particularly low point in the band's recording career.

'But where's Mark? What did he say about Mark?' Richard asked her.

'He said he's keeping Mark with him until he gets his money.'

'We have to go to the police! This is extortion!' Richard cried.

The fear was still in his voice but now there was anger too, and he looked as if he was about to blow a valve. Emma put her hands on his shoulders and went on tiptoe to kiss him lightly on the lips.

'We can't go to the police, darling. What about Mark? If anything did happen to him –'

'Don't even say that!' Richard groaned.

He looked round and saw me as if for the first time. Shiny with pomade, his hair was combed into a sharp chevron, the parting a white scar running back from his red-brown forehead.

'I can't believe you've gone and wasted money doing up this bloody room,' he snapped at her.

She looked startled and with good reason. After all, the deal seemed perfectly clear-cut: Emma would make him feel young and Richard would make her feel wealthy.

'You don't even like entertaining!' he cried. 'Remember the last dinner party we had?'

'Let's not get into this now, darling,' she said, with a glance in my direction.

Richard rolled his thick shoulders and it amazed me that he could bicker with his wife when he had reason to believe his son was in danger, but maybe the threat to Mark was just too distressing for him to face. The plates he was spinning had started to wobble and drop.

'Sorry, darling. Forgive me. Let's go and call the police.'

'No! We can't risk it. They might be watching the house!'

She looked terrified. I'd never seen her so worked up, not even during the Pigeon White crisis, and I couldn't understand why she was so adamant they didn't call the police. Emma and her husband headed for the door and I listened to their conversation as they made their way up the stairs.

'But I thought you said he sounded Jamaican,' Richard said. 'I don't see anyone sophisticated behind this. It's more likely to be some petty crook acting alone.'

'No way. Absolutely not. He sounded very on top of it, very professional. I think you should just give them the bloody stamps.'

On the first floor a door scraped across fitted carpet and closed.

I was scared stiff that they'd be able to trace a second call to Jeff's number and I spent a bad hour trying to stop myself sicking up my guts. When I finally gave in and went to the tiny bathroom under the stairs to get it over with, I heard raised voices. It sounded as if Emma and Richard were arguing, but even with my ear Dumboed forward and the door ajar, I couldn't make out any individual words. I puked and waited for the spasms to die down, staring at a framed photo of Emma at a charity gala.

Not a single blonde hair was out of place but I detected a cheated look on her face, as if she'd just begun to realize the price for entry into the land of obscene wealth. Beside it hung a small framed playbill for a production of *A Long Day's Journey into Night* in Sydney, Australia. As Emma Coates she'd taken the part of Cathleen. Prior to the Pigeon White crisis she'd sat around one afternoon while I worked, smoking her low-tar cigarettes as she retailed low-interest anecdotes from her uneventful acting career, and by five o'clock I'd begun to think that hairdressers were underpaid. Half hidden behind the curtain was a picture of Richard in his thirties. Resembling a young Mark Thatcher, he was standing in a garden beside a starved-looking brunette with big scared eyes and a plump frowning child. This was Mark, snapped between his dead mother and Richard in a soft-grained family group. Richard seemed to want no part of it and Mark looked equally uncomfortable as his mother's fingers fed the current of her neurosis directly into his neck. I had to presume he'd saved his smiles for Ildikó.

When the phone rang again at four o'clock, cold hands used my intestines for Plasticine. I expected to be collared any minute, but mercifully nothing came of the call. It could have been anyone and half an hour later I'd even begun to relax a little as I removed bands of masking tape from the light switches and the shelves. Then I heard someone behind me and I nearly snapped the fat cable right then and there. It was Emma, looking drained and agitated. I had no idea how long she'd been watching me.

'Any news?' I asked.

Her mouth was set hard and I was petrified she'd connected me to the calls.

'Richard spoke to him,' she said.

'Is Mark OK?'

She shrugged, unwilling to be drawn. I wanted to find out if Richard had called the police but I couldn't think of a way to frame the question in a natural way.

'Are you nearly finished for the day?' she asked.

I had the impression that she wanted me out of the house and it suited me fine. I was desperate to stop Phil from doing any more harm.

'Yes, just about. I don't suppose there's any chance you managed to get to the bank?'

She looked at me as if I was mad.

'Not with everything that's happened. You'll have to wait until tomorrow.'

Emma went back upstairs and ten minutes later I carried my tool-bag out into the refrigerated street. The driver's door of the van was unlocked. Surprised at my negligence, I climbed inside and saw a shadow move against the rear window. There was someone in the back of the van.

9

It was Phil, hunched on a tarpaulin.

'What are you fucking doing?' I snarled.

'Get in. They're watching us!'

He was pointing to the Bowrings' house through the rear window and I saw a figure behind the net curtains of the first-floor drawing room. It looked like Richard. Did he suspect me? I had to get us away from there. Luckily the engine started first time.

'You fucking stupid idiot!' I shouted at him. 'How could you?'

The job with Emma might have led on to more lucrative work but now he'd jeopardized all that and more. I hated Phil then, the way I'd hated him when the band fell apart, with a deep loathing. He clawed at my shoulder, excited and somehow surprised at my reaction.

'Hang on, Andy. This was your idea! I only did what you said.'

'You prat, I was kidding! Richard's calling it extortion.'

Phil pulled his tobacco out of his pocket.

'Mind if I, er?'

'Smoke? I don't give a shit if you burn. You didn't use Jeff's phone did you?'

'Mark's mobile. I've got it with me.'

He looked so pleased with himself that I wanted to throttle him.

'Where's Mark?'

'Back at Jeff's.'

Phil clambered over into the front passenger seat clutching a stretched-out wire coat hanger as I pulled out into the stop-go chicken-run of Marylebone Road, heading west.

'And Sara?' I asked.

'She was still asleep when I left. Look, I've just told Richard to leave the stamps in the WH Smith at Marylebone Station. I've got to be sure he hasn't told the police.'

'Why the fuck wouldn't he?'

It seemed the obvious thing for him to do. I would have. Richard may have been a lousy client, but he was still Mark's father and I remembered the fear in his voice.

'Because he can't risk Mark talking,' said Phil. 'Not with him creaming Mark's trust fund.'

'That's all bollocks!'

'I don't think so. You should've heard him on the phone. He was shitting himself. Look, the way I see it, we pick up the stamps and then we tell Mark it didn't work out. And we'll split the money we get, you and me.'

'You berk! You think I'm going to help you? They know me!'

'Richard knows me too. He met me with you, remember? So you're involved whether you like it or not.'

A tight pocket of air pressed up in my chest and my heart rate doubled. I caught Phil's eye and he sucked at his cheap teeth. When he spoke again, his words came out as dull and flat as a talking clock.

'It's up to you,' he said. 'But I'm going through with this and you're in it whether you help or not.'

'You slimy fucking little maggot! That's blackmail!'

'Like I said, it was your idea.'

The blood in my legs set like hair gel.

'It'll be crowded in the store at five,' Phil said. 'The rush hour. I told Richard to put the stamp album in a white carrier bag and leave it by a magazine rack. I'll go in and pick it up. I just need you to keep an eye out.'

I pulled to a stop by a phone booth near Madame Tussaud's.

'What are you doing? he asked.

'I'm calling the police.'

'You can't do that!'

'Oh no?'

Phil stared at me with red round pigeon eyes. I remembered the time he'd blown the petrol money for our tour van, a van even less salubrious than the one in which we now sat, and I curbed the same urge to hit him.

'Wait. All right, I'll do it alone,' he said. 'If I get caught, I'll leave you out of it. Honest. Look, this is my last chance. It's all I've got. If it goes wrong, I'll say I planned it all myself.'

'I can't let you do that.'

His features tightened until his face looked small and hateful. I got out of the van, opened the passenger door, and dragged him on to the pavement.

'Fuck you, Phil,' I shouted in his face. 'Go fuck your life up.'

Beneath the canopy of Madame Tussaud's the queue of tourists came to sudden life in the hope that we'd make a further spectacle of ourselves, but I drove away and left Phil shouting at me as he shrank in the side mirror. My knuckles were white on a steering wheel as thin as wire. I was hoping he got caught. That he'd get ten years. I had nothing to fear. It was nothing to do with me. But as I headed back to Kilburn the doubts stacked up in my mind like a week's worth of washing-up. If the police caught

Phil he'd give me up as co-conspirator without a second thought. I cursed him and checked my watch. It was just before five. Starting to panic, I made an illegal U-turn. I had to stop him.

Opposite Marylebone Station I found an empty meter bay with twenty free minutes on it and I locked the van and ran on to the station concourse. Phil was sitting on a red circular seating module opposite WH Smith, drinking from a gold can of Carlsberg for Danish courage and peering at the passers-by over the top of the *Evening Standard*. He looked scared out of his mind. A pair of policemen stood in front of a pub in the corner of the station. They were speaking to a young woman wearing jeans, a young woman who could have been a tourist asking for directions. Or a plain-clothes policewoman waiting to finger Phil when he picked up the carrier bag. My throat tightened as the woman headed into WH Smith, passing right by Phil, and the uniformed couple followed her to dawdle by a small coffee bar in the middle of the concourse. I didn't dare approach Phil. I was breathing but it didn't feel as if any oxygen was getting into my bloodstream. I felt horribly exposed – a cockroach caught in the middle of a kitchen floor by the flick of a light switch, yearning for the safety of the dust and shadows beneath the fridge. I saw a Photo-me booth, ducked inside and pulled the curtain across to leave a slit through which I could observe both Phil and the entrance to WH Smith. Putting change into the machine, I prayed that Phil would look round, see the police and back off.

I checked my watch. It was 5.05. Whoomph! The first camera flash went off in my face and the shock it delivered could well have been enough to stop Richard's heart for good. There was no sign of him. The Tannoy quacked out a list of stops and commuters flowed past the booth, blocking my view of WH Smith, but I saw the police couple go over to brace a black man. Phil was completely rigid, paralysed with fears of his own, and then he suddenly sat forward. I followed his gaze and saw Richard Bowring striding into WH Smith.

Whoomph! Richard was wrapped in a pale raincoat and he carried a paler carrier bag. I was amazed that Emma had persuaded him to deliver the stamps. It was a set-up. They'd told the police! Seconds later he emerged and headed for the exit without the bag or a backward glance. As soon as Richard was out of sight, Phil stood up with his shoulders hunched around his ears. Even at a distance of thirty feet I could feel the fear coming off him. He scratched the top of his head, feigning nonchalance, and looked right-left-right to scan the concourse.

Whoomph! Another heart-stopping blaze of halogen Tippexed my world.

Someone was watching Phil, a tall young man with an elongated face who stood by the coffee bar. He was wearing a suit and tie and looked about twenty-five, not long out of police college. I noticed him only because he turned away when Phil looked at him. Phil took a step towards WH Smith and Long-face moved from the coffee bar to follow him, threading a path through the stream of commuters. When the lights flashed for the fourth and final time, I emerged from the cubicle and pretended to wait for my photos. A potential have-a-go hero lounged by the door to WH Smith, a jock in a suit with a rugby-club neck. Phil would drag us all down with him. I saw Sara behind prison bars and, without giving myself time to think, I body-swerved through the crowd towards WH Smith. I had to get Phil out of there before he had time to pick up the carrier bag.

I walked into WH Smith with sand-papered senses. The store was hot and the heated air smelt of electronics. It was quiet – just the rustle of clothing, the chug-whir of the till and a murmured apology for an unwitting nudge. The queue for the till curled back into the store and I pushed my way through it to see Phil, a black crow silhouetted against a mosaic of magazine covers, picking over the carcass of a music paper. I moved along the aisle and nearly bumped into Long-face. I circled him and picked up a book that sought to explain what the pyramid-builders had really been up to. Long-face kept an eye on Phil while pretending to examine some padded envelopes. A white carrier bag was propped against the lower shelf of a magazine display. Phil was inching himself down the rack towards it and I could feel the net closing in on both of us, ready to snag our gills in its web. I went to the end of the magazine rack, intending to draw a warning finger across my throat when Phil looked my way. But he didn't. I picked up a computer magazine and moved closer to him, keeping my back to Long-face, who was about ten feet away. I coughed. Phil looked round at me.

'The police are here!' I rasped.

The music paper shook in his hands.

'Where?' he whispered.

'Right behind you. Just go. Not to Jeff's. Go home,' I said, trying to keep a rising terror out of my voice.

Reracking the computer magazine, I sneaked a glance and saw Long-face step out from behind the stationery display to block Phil's path. He was brandishing a black notebook. Phil bunched his shoulders, feinted left and went right, barging Long-face into a display stand before sprinting off across the concourse. People stopped and stared. I expected Long-face to give chase but he stayed put, presumably leaving it to the uniformed clones. Then he turned my way.

Long-face looked straight at me and his face lit up. I couldn't move. He bared his teeth in something like a smile.

It was over. Crushed like a cubed car, I was oddly calm and even found the time to speculate as to what courses would be available to me in prison before Long-face laid a hand on my arm.

'Wow,' he said. 'I can't believe it! You're Andy Hayes, aren't you? I saw you play Falmouth on my eighteenth birthday! You signed my copy of "Big Ben"!'

It took me a moment to get it, then I laughed out loud. Long-face was just a mad fan.

'I've got everything you released!' he cried.

I wanted to hug him, even though it represented a negligible investment.

Equally ecstatic, Long-face reached into his pocket for a pen and presented me with his notebook. At his request I signed it 'To Sean'. Commuters were looking at us and I searched their faces for the young woman in the jeans, but she was nowhere to be seen. As I headed for the street, Sean asked me why Phil had run off and, reaching, I floated the unlikely explanation that Phil was chronically shy and lived in terror of his ever-persistent fan-base.

'You know, Phil and I share the same birthday,' Sean said.

'Lucky you,' I replied.

As soon as I'd slipped the noose of Sean's sociability, tension fell away in wobbling chunks of uncontrollable laughter. Taxi drivers were dropping off their passengers and I trotted past them, in no hurry to tell anyone about the true nature of Sean's observances. I realized I'd do better to let Mark think that the police were on to him and Phil, so that he'd leave Jeff's and go to ground until I'd finished the job at his dad's house. Giddy with relief and adrenalin, I climbed into the van, but no sooner had I shut the door than I saw a way to make things right. I had to fetch the carrier bag from WH Smith and return the stamps to Richard. Sara knew him and we would go to see him together and explain what had happened. Everything would work out fine.

I went back to the store and headed straight for the magazine racks. I was worried that a career bag-snatcher might have taken the carrier but it was still in place, so I picked it up and walked out of the store with my heart trying to punch its way out of my chest. No one gave chase and, once inside the van, I removed the album from the bag, excited as a kid with a shoplifting haul.

Rain flowed down the windscreen and the streetlight projected it on to the album, bathing the pale leather binding with the illusion of molten plastic. The pigskin cover was stamped with the initials MRB and the album contained two dozen cellophane sleeves displaying blocks of stamps carefully mounted on stiff cardboard. Rainwater leaked into the van from the top of the window seal to drip on my thigh and when I pushed the rubber trim back in place it felt soft and sticky enough to take a fingerprint. I held one of the pages up to the streetlight and inspected the multiple faces of a dead white male with a jutting beard. In the aquarium light the stamps were something of a disappointment. They must have meant so much to Mark, but without his collector's enthusiasm they were just scraps of old paper and glue. Hundreds of Sicilians see the tears of a plaster Madonna but the reporter from *Time* magazine arrives by helicopter and sees nothing at all. I thought about returning the album to Richard straight away, without taking Sara with me. And if I'd done that I'd have saved myself a whole heap of trouble. Instead I stuffed the album under my seat and drove back to Jeff's in the hope that she was still there with Mark.

10

Pulling into Jeff's square, I saw that the lights were on in the flat. When I felt beneath my seat for the album, I discovered that the lining had come unstitched, so I ran two fingers along the seam to open it up some more and wedged the stamp album between the cloth and the metal frame that housed the springs. Then I dashed through the rain into Jeff's building. My organs sagged in my torso as the lift hoisted me fifty feet into the air, and as soon as the doors sucked apart on the fourth floor I heard music: Jamiroquai at full volume, the aural equivalent of a kid tagging the Botticelli Venus with a marker pen.

Mark was dancing with his eyes closed in the middle of the living room, his upper teeth squeezed down on his lower lip in the classic white man's overbite. The yellow rug had been rolled back against the wall and I saw that the red-wine spill from the previous night had seeped right through to the hessian underlay, the way blood from a cut fills the gauze grid of a bandage. There was no sign of Sara. I called Mark's name but he didn't hear me, so I went to the CD player and killed the power. He turned, taking an extra step to steady himself as his eyes hauled me into focus, hopelessly drunk. I decided to revert to my original plan and tell him that the police had been at the station, so that he'd clear out of the flat.

'Andy. Uh, hey, d'you get them?'

'No. The police were there,' I lied.

Mark was stunned and I could almost taste the soured urgency of his hopes. Another empty vodka bottle lay by his feet on the wooden floor, pointing at thin air. Breathing hard, Mark tottered towards me.

'He told the police? Dad told the police?'

'Looks that way. You'd better get out of here.'

Something went still inside him.

'I s'pose Sara must've called him then,' he said.

'Where is she?' I asked. He was so distracted that I had to repeat the question.

'She just left,' he mumbled. 'We had a fight.'

I grabbed him by the front of his shirt, the green and yellow stripes twisting tight as earth wire in my fists. As his eyes opened up I saw cream-coloured clouds at the perimeter from which red bolts forked towards the irises.

'What d'you mean, a fight?'

'I didn't touch her!' he said. 'She'd heard Phil make the call to Dad, so I just told her he'd gone to fetch my stamps for me and – well, she wanted to tell Dad. I had to stop her and that's why I told her you were in on it. Helping us. Actually, I was thinking because she likes you she wouldn't make the call. But it didn't make any difference.'

A chill ran over my skin and I wanted to throw Mark off the balcony. Sara thought I was involved. Feeling sick, I asked Mark for her phone number. He said he'd lost his address book, so I went to see if she'd left a note for me in my room. The bed had been made but there was no message. Spitting feathers, I went into the kitchen and rang directory inquiries to ask for Sara Carberry's number in Dalston, only to find there was no listing. I then asked for Dean's number, but of course Dean, being a self-aggrandizing prick, had made himself ex-directory. I told myself to calm down. All I had to do was to find Sara, tell her what had really happened and then the two of us could return the stamps to Richard.

Back in the living room I found Mark mewling, holding the blister pack of Dexedrine.

'You should clear out of here,' I said. 'The police could be round any minute.'

'But I've nowhere to go! My father's never loved me! That's why he didn't hand over the stamps! Don't you see?'

With the staring eyes of a drunk turned pensive, Mark blamed everything on Richard. It was the one fixed point in his personality.

'I'm going to go to Regent's Park and have it out with him,' he said.

'Hey, hang on. That's not such a good idea.'

I started to panic, because if Mark got to Richard before me I'd be in even deeper trouble. After all, the stamps were still in my van. Mark would return to his private clinic and Phil and I would end up in some rather more public prison. Mark had been drinking and popping enough pills to warrant the application of a Hazchem symbol to the back of his shirt, but he still picked up on my anxiety about what he'd say to Richard. And of course he took it the wrong way.

'God, I see it all!' he snarled. 'You're working for my father! You've been against me from the start.'

Mark wasn't on the edge, he was over it, arms and legs flailing in midair. I couldn't handle him alone.

'You got the stamps too, didn't you?' he bleated. 'You've been lying! You're trying to cheat me. It was your idea to make the call in the first place, Andy! I'm going to tell my father that it was all your idea!'

His paranoia was clacking away in a domino-run and I badly needed Phil's help.

I went to the kitchen and phoned him, but a taped voice told me that his number was 'unavailable' and I realized that I'd have to go to his flat in Hammersmith to fetch him. When I returned to the sitting room, Mark was on the sofa, weeping brattish tears.

'Phil's at his place by now. I could give you a lift over there if you like,' I said.

Mark scowled at me and said that he wasn't going anywhere. From the new electricity in his eyes it looked as if the Dexedrine was reclaiming command of his central nervous system. I knew I had to call Richard and tell him everything, with or without Sara, so I went to the kitchen to dial the Bowrings' number. Mark followed me and demanded to know who I was calling.

'Your father,' I said.

'No!' he yelled.

Mark gave me a shove and I fell backwards into a kitchen unit, banging it hard with my hip. He grabbed the phone and ripped it clean off the wall, screws and plastic plugs included. Picking myself up, I flashed on the phone's ghost blow-print – the outline of the case pale against the much-fingered surrounding paintwork. Mark yanked at the cord until it broke and then he hurled the phone across the room at me, the set and receiver stretching their coiled connecting cord into a twirling bolas. I ducked as the phone-set dented the microwave a millisecond before the receiver clanged against the bread bin. Mark came and hit me hard in the stomach. It knocked the wind right out of me and I bent double as he clubbed me with his fists. I blundered forward and pushed him and he fell sideways, hitting the edge of the fridge with his face. Blood ran out of his nose and across his cheek, dark and viscous, as if it had originated deep within his body. He collapsed on the floor, rubbing tears and blood into his face.

I stumbled to the bedroom and discovered that the phone in there no longer worked. Somehow I had to call Richard. The last thing I wanted was to leave Mark alone in the flat but I had no choice, so I hobbled down the stairs and headed for the phone box on the corner, carrying a leaden stitch from Mark's punch. Each step took an effort of will.

A teenager in snow-boarding clothes was using the phone and I waited in torment for a couple of minutes, trying to stem an oozing panic about Sara. Eventually I lost patience and tapped on the window. Taking this as a threat to his fledgling manhood, the kid shot me a dirty look and jangled a handful of change in my face before turning his back on me. I crossed the square to use the pay-phone in the hotel lobby and found a Scandinavian woman trying to alter her family's travel arrangements in her pulverized English. She had enough coins piled on the shelf in front of her to make a reasonable maquette of Manhattan. In despair I returned to the booth on the corner. The teenager was still in there, and I was ready to smash straight through the glass and kick the spots off his face by the time he finally hung up. I pushed past him and grabbed the dangling receiver, only to discover that I had no silver or pound coins among the jumble of keys and coppers in my pocket. There were no notes in my wallet either.

Swearing out loud, I headed for the bank on the main road, where I keyed in my Personal Identification Number with a rare fluency. Nothing happened. I pressed the numbers again and focused on the crescents of grime that had collected on the metal mounting that surrounded the black buttons. The screen informed me that I'd entered my number incorrectly. I thought I'd go crazy. Mark could have burnt Jeff's flat down or been half-way to Regent's Park by now. This time I stabbed the buttons hard, holding them down until the pressure bleached my fingernail. Bonanza. The machine doled out three frayed ten-pound notes. I broke one of them in the off-licence and ran back to the booth. As I dialled the Bowrings' number for the second time, I realized I could have made a reverse-charge call through the operator and saved myself ten or twelve minutes.

Ildikó answered the phone. She sounded frightened.

'Hi,' I said. 'It's Andy. Is Mr Richard there?'

She told me that he was out, and so was Emma.

Where were they?

'Is things the matter?' she asked.

I couldn't tell Ildikó what had happened. I needed to speak to Richard in person.

'No. No, it's nothing important. Just that I might be in a bit late tomorrow. I've got to pick some stuff up. Some paint. OK?'

I hung up. The lights were out in Jeff's flat and I was hoping Mark had gone when I saw a low-slung sports car on the north side of the square. It looked like Richard's testosterone patch of a vehicle, but it was hard to tell the colour given the muddying effect of the streetlight. The car came in my direction, the engine's growl protesting its owner's enduring vitality. I hid behind a Jeep and as the car pulled alongside I glanced down at the driver's seat (or rather the driver's mattress), but the angle was too acute and I glimpsed only a blurred hand on the wheel. As the car pulled away I noted the last three letters of the number plate: JBK, the letters calling to mind Jay Bloody Kay, the charmless hatted gnome who fronted Jamiroquai. A split second later the car disappeared on to the main road and I told myself I was getting as paranoid as Mark. Hundreds of menopausal Sting fans bought cars like that every day.

When I got back to Jeff's flat I discovered Mark's dead body.

11

I looked out through the fish-eye Judas to see Phil's giant black pupil and white spinnaker of a nose. When I opened the door he came through in a rush, and my legs were shaking so much that I had to support myself against the wall. I tried to speak but my tongue wouldn't work. Phil saw the change in me, grabbed my arm and shook it.

'What is it?' he asked. 'What's wrong?'

I could only point to the living room. Phil went through and when he saw the back of Mark's head, he called his name just as I'd done. Then he walked round the sofa, stepping over the loose CDs that covered the floor like big sequins. When he saw Mark's face, he gulped and searched his wrist for a pulse. Again, just as I'd done.

'It's not there,' I said.

Phil dropped Mark's forearm and took a couple of steps backwards, treading carefully like an old man on an icy pavement.

'Is he dead?' he asked, his face a slide-area.

I nodded.

'What happened?'

'He killed himself. With all those pills. The bottle's empty. He was in a bad way when I left him.'

As I spoke the words my stomach turned cold. Had our tussle pushed Mark over the edge? Christ, had the bang against the fridge given him a brain haemorrhage? The body lay there with its electricity cut off, freeze-framed, and the face began to look as if it had been sculpted from clay by an unfeeling technician. Mark's fat legs poked straight out in front of him.

Phil was shaking, trying to grapple with the brute fact of his death. Observing the shock take hold of Phil, my own symptoms were assuaged and I became transfixed by a sticking plaster on the index finger of Mark's right hand. The pink cloth was wrapped around the lower joint and the plaster had rolled back at the edge to reveal a rim of gum darkened with dirt, but infection no longer posed a threat. In the palm of this dead man's hand there was a lifeline carved long and deep, all the way to the heel, and it was one in the eye for the palmistry business.

'There's blood on your chin,' Phil said.

Puzzled, I went to the mirror in the hall. It was true. There was a red smear at the side of my mouth. I'd bitten into my lip without noticing and the lip had swollen. I looked pale and criminal. Mug-shot. I wiped the blood away with the back of my hand. When I looked round, Phil was frowning at me from the doorway. The hall was narrow and the walls seemed to press in even closer.

'I must've bitten my lip. When I found him,' I said.

Phil dragged his eyes from my face to Mark's body and back again. I began to hyperventilate.

'What are you looking at me like that for?' I asked.

Phil sucked on his new teeth. Again I saw Mark's head smash against the fridge and the blood trickle out of his nose, but I tried to push the pictures aside. The blood had gone from his face so Mark must have had time to clean himself up before the pills worked.

'Listen,' I said. 'I went out to make a call and when I got back Mark was dead.'

'Why didn't you just make the call from here?' Phil asked.

'Mark went mental and tore the phone off the wall. He thought I was working for his dad. I mean, you know. That I'd told Richard what you were up to.'

'And did you?'

'I was going to but he was out, probably looking for his son. Anyway, where've you been? I thought you were going back to your place.'

'How could I? I left my keys here,' Phil said. 'And I had to give the police the slip. I was lucky to get away.'

'God, if I hadn't left him though. If I'd stayed –'

Tears scorched my eyes and Phil led me back into the living room. He slumped down on the armchair and hugged his knees.

'I can't fucking believe this!' he wailed.

As Phil worked himself up I felt calmer, as though we were playing pass-the-parcel with hysteria. It had started to hit him and he extracted the packet of Dexedrine from the mess on the coffee table.

'I don't think we should go moving anything around,' I said.

'Why not?'

'Well, the police –'

He leapt from the armchair.

'Forget the police! If we tell the police we go to prison. We're that far away as it is,' Phil said. 'Richard'll just say we abducted him. They'll be looking for scapegoats.'

'What about Sara?'

'Don't be a moron! We can't tell anyone about this!'

I still hadn't taken in what had happened. I was in shock.

'So what do we do?' I asked.

Phil looked over at the corpse, as if he expected Mark to

chip in with an idea of his own, and then he looked me in the eye.

'We get rid of the body,' he said.

I felt sick.

'That's crazy,' I said. 'It's an overdose. It's not our fault. We can go to the police.'

'You'd get ten years!' Phil snapped. 'How long d'you think it'd take them to tie us to the phone calls? Even with their clear-up rate? I mean, look at us! I've got a record for theft, you're a dole cheat. We have to dump the body. We've no choice.'

I was struck by his vehemence on the subject of the police. It reminded me of Emma earlier in the day.

'But a post-mortem would put us in the clear,' I said.

'No fucking way!'

I thought I was going mad.

'But I didn't bloody kill him!' I shouted. 'Why should I move the body? It doesn't make any sense! Let's call the police!'

He braced me against the wall.

'You're losing it, Andy,' he said. 'Let me do the thinking, yeah? Trust me.'

He wasn't going to budge an inch on the matter and I was scared that he'd just walk out if I didn't agree. After all, I had the keys to the flat and I'd taken the stamps. And I'd smacked Mark's head against the fridge.

'Yes, all right. I guess so.'

'Where's Sara?' he asked.

'Mark said she got up after you left. She'd heard you make the call, though. She had a row with Mark and then she must have phoned Richard. I think I just saw him outside driving off in his car.'

My earlier suspicions now seemed more than justified.

Phil's face went runny for a second and then he shrugged it off.

'You saw a car like his,' he said.

'Well, I –'

'All right, so what if she did phone him? So what if he even came round here? He'd have pressed the buzzer and there'd've been no reply.'

'I tell you –'

'More reason to get rid of the body. Look, Andy. Let's get one thing straight. The law's for people like Richard Bowring. We just say Mark left here in a state and that's all we know. If it comes to it, Sara'll back us up that he was in on the whole thing. With the stamp album.'

'What if we're caught moving the body?' I asked.

Phil shrugged again and the gesture irritated me. He'd made up his mind about what to do and now he wasn't going to entertain any objections.

'We're screwed if we don't,' he said. 'We'll just dump him. Dump him in the river.'

As I pictured Phil and me on a bridge struggling to throw Mark's dead and inexpertly weighted body over a parapet, I felt sick again. If I'd taken a minute to think about it, I'd have realized that Phil was talking rubbish, and that we had no choice but to go to the police. However, the bile table rose in my chest and I rushed to the bathroom.

Stomach juice paint-strippered my throat as I braced myself over the pan and gagged. Phil stayed away, having just enough remaining good sense to leave me to it. Afterwards I washed my hands and face, struggling to snuff the image of Mark's dead body from the inside of my eyelids. Everything felt hollow and unreal in Jeff's bright bathroom. I started humming, but then Mark's dead face came back to me again with its drying fish-eyes and I heaved until it felt as if my body was turning itself inside out. Insensible to further pain, I cleaned my teeth so vigorously that my gums bled red froth, and I remember the flow of dental pink water distorting the shape of the chrome plughole.

I don't know how long I spent in the bathroom, but when I returned to the living room there was no sign of Phil. I was terrified that he'd done a runner, but then I heard him talking to himself in the kitchen. Had the discovery of Mark's body cracked his mind? When I went in there, I found him saying goodbye to someone on Mark's mobile phone. I asked him who he'd been speaking to, hoping against hope that he'd say Sara.

'Justin. Justin my cousin,' he said. 'He's going to help us.'

'You told Justin about this? I don't believe it! He's a nutter!'

Justin was an unpredictable maniac whose tenuous grip on reality had been further loosened by hard drugs. Difficult drugs. He'd been sacked from the European leg of our final tour for hospitalizing a fan in the lobby of our hotel. I remembered seeing Justin at Dean's party.

'He's straightened himself out now,' said Phil. 'Got a wife and kids. He works as a butcher with his uncle in Norwood.'

'So what the fuck did you call him for?'

'Look, we had a chat at Dean's, right? And it happens, he mentioned he could get rid of a body. He was very particular about his clientele. "No women, nothing kinky." His exact words. Come on, Andy. Justin's family and it's our best chance.'

'You twit, he was just showing off,' I said.

'That's what I thought at first, but he said he does it all

the time. He's not some timid little wanker like you. And have you got a better plan?'

With a normal overdose you'd just dump the corpse on some waste ground or leave it in the bath. At least that had been the standard operating procedure in the rock biographies I'd read as a teenager. However, the fake abduction ruled that out according to Phil. It may have been a strip of Dentotape that he offered but it felt like a straw and I badly needed something to clutch right then. I remembered Justin taking a load of us to a drinking club in Lewisham, and although he'd spent most of the evening making tedious boasts of his connections with police and criminal circles in south-east London, these claims had turned out to be legitimate. North Ken had been charged with drink-driving soon afterwards and Justin had passed six grand in cash to a bent solicitor on Ken's behalf so that the police would lose the paperwork. As in the Stephen Lawrence business, the case never went to trial. On balance, it was just possible that Justin could get rid of a body, but if he was telling the truth about his new sideline, he was betting heavily against the existence of St Peter or at least on a very lax door policy.

'Come on, Andy. It'll be all right,' said Phil. 'We're going to meet him at a pub in Norwood. The butcher's shop's just up the road.'

It sounded shaky, but I made the decision to go along with it and attempted to bury myself in the detail.

'What does he plan to do with the body?' I asked.

'Carcasses. Cows and pigs. You know. Sheep. They're carting it off all the time. No one's going to notice a few stray bits of Mark in with that lot.'

The image sank in: animal-rights footage and atrocity newsreel spliced together in the steel maw of a garbage truck. I felt sick and repaired once more to the bathroom. When I was finished, I went back to the kitchen.

'I just can't go through with this,' I said.

'You'll be fine. It'll be over before you know it. Come on.'

I followed Phil into the living room, praying Mark's body would have disappeared. It hadn't. Phil went straight over and tried to lift it.

'Here, give us a hand, will you?'

I stood back. Phil was trying to act as if handling a corpse was nothing special, but he was overdoing it, heightening my sense of a mushrooming unreality.

'Get a grip, Andy. This is just scrap human remains. It's not a person any more, all right? It's evidence. Remember that.'

I was being bulldozed and I needed time to think. Phil sighed and let Mark's body slump back down on the sofa. I felt angry and confused, and I pinned it on Phil for making the call without consulting me. I asked him how much money Justin wanted.

'Three hundred.'

'Where are we going to get that?' I asked.

'Well, I haven't got it.'

'So I'm paying, am I?'

'Fuck it, we're facing ten years and you're worried about three hundred quid? I'm trying to get us out of this mess, but if you have any better ideas then tell me! I'm all ears. Because I could just leave you to deal with this on your own. I mean, what's stopping me? It's not like Jeff loaned the place to me. But I've stuck around, haven't I? Unlike your bloody girlfriend.'

He had a point. I knew I was lost if he walked out and I found myself on the brink of a huge panic attack. I had no option but surrender, so I raised my arms and walked towards the enemy lines.

'OK, you're right,' I said. 'I just hope Justin'll do it.'

'He didn't want to talk about it on the mobile but yeah, he'll do it. We've just got to get it down there.'

I flinched at this repeated use of the neuter. To me Mark was still very much around, like an unlucky Swede you met once in Munich who comes to London and needs a place to stay.

'How do we get him to Norwood?' I asked.

Phil scratched the beginnings of a scratchy new beard.

'We'll take him down in the lift when it's all quiet. Prop him up between us, put him in the van and go. You'd better park it up at the front of the building.'

When I looked down from the balcony I saw that the square was rammed with cars as usual, so there was no choice but to double-park and risk being clamped. Seldom had the lack of an integrated transport strategy for London struck me so forcibly. There were still pedestrians in the square and it would be touch and go getting Mark past them without being spotted, but when I went back inside I had an idea.

'We could take him down in the service lift,' I said. 'No one uses it at night. And it comes out behind the building.'

Phil agreed and when I went to move the van, the lift made a slow dive straight down to G, laying nausea over nausea in a queasy lasagne. Out in the square, tourists disembarked from a purple coach in front of the hotel and private cars kerb-crawled the square in search of sex or parking places. It felt like normality and I breathed a few litres of the cold night air before moving the van to the narrow street at the back of the building. I parked right by the loading bay. When I returned to the flat, Phil clapped me on the back as if I'd just played an unexpectedly good round of golf, but his front of nineteenth-hole conviviality was given the lie by a vein at his temple that tapped out his underlying distress. It pulsed proud of the bone, squiggly as a bungee cord on the upswing.

'I really don't think I can handle this,' I said. Something had seized up inside me.

'Course you can. When it's over just lock it all away. After a while it'll feel like it happened to someone else.'

'I doubt that, Phil. I really doubt that.'

'Remember, we didn't kill him. We're just saving our skins.'

We drank whisky and Phil poured some of it down Mark's shirt front. If anyone saw him, we hoped they'd catch a whiff and assume he was drunk. Then Phil thumbed down Mark's eyelids and pulled his curly hair forward over his cheeks. The rings around the eyes had darkened, as if Mark had somehow squeezed yet another heavy night into the past half-hour. It took an enormous effort to help Phil lift him. Following his lead, I knelt on the sofa to place Mark's arm round my shoulder. Mark's hand felt hot, hotter than mine, and this startled me because I'd have expected it to have cooled down. Later I was told that the body heats up right after death, that the cells keep working in an effect known as post-mortem caloricity.

We had the body half-way up from the sofa when Mark burped loudly.

I sprang back in shock and waited for the zombie to open his eyes and regain the gift of speech. Phil took a cautious step in Mark's direction and forced himself to lift the lid on a dead eye.

'It's all right. It's only gas,' said Phil. 'Escaping gas. Nothing to worry about.'

I took a few deep breaths. Mark's body was heavy, but we managed to lift him up between us and walked him across the room without too much trouble, dragging his feet over the wooden floor. Mark was still supple but his head was stuck over to one side and I pointed this out to Phil.

'It's no bad thing,' said Phil. 'With his hair pushed forward no one can see his face.'

We propped Mark against the wall in the hallway and the three of us were reflected in the mirror as a grainy police line-up. In contrast to Phil and me, Mark looked enviably peaceful. I opened the door on an empty landing, ran the length of it and pressed the down button beside the service lift. I was ready to slap on an insincere smile and say I was a decorator working late if anyone challenged me, but the lift was empty. We dragged Mark along the landing and bundled him inside, the pitted grey doors hissing together to enclose us as quietly as quicksand. I had a sudden sense that I'd lost something valuable, something I'd never recover, the way I used to feel before going on stage.

This was the most dangerous part. If anyone got a good close-range look at Mark, it would all be over, because although we hadn't killed him, we were behaving exactly as if we had. There was an unpleasant bounce, a gallows drop, as the lift settled on the ground floor. Finding ourselves in a short corridor, we eased Mark through some push-bar doors and dragged him down the steps. The street was deserted and I held the body upright while Phil opened the back of the van. Mark seemed even heavier than he had in the flat and I felt my muscles tear as I struggled to support him single-handedly against the wall. We lifted his body inside the van and then Phil hurled a dustsheet over him. Climbing in behind the wheel, I turned the key in the ignition with my fingers crossed, but luckily the van started on cue and as we drove off the fear settled down to ripple through me in neat regular waves.

12

High tension cheese-wired down through my neck and shoulders as I fed the van into the log-run of Park Lane, aware that the slightest infraction of the Highway Code could be enough to put us in jail. I drove south from Tyburn Gate at 30 m.p.h., jolted by the beeps of various discourtesy cars. In the passenger seat Phil chewed at a stick of gum, his jaw muscles knotting with each chomp, and he nimmed his knee up and down in the footwell. When I turned too fast at Hyde Park Corner, Mark's body slid across the floor behind us and I looked at the rear-view mirror, terrorized by the thought that his living-dead face was about to pop up behind me.

The instant my eyes were off the road we drifted across some hatched lane markings. Phil yelled and I yanked us back on track, advising him that I already had one (in fact the ultimate) back-seat driver. The corpse directed our every move, and Phil twisted in his seat to check that it was still covered by the dustsheet. Mark had a more forceful presence dead than alive and I could hear his voice in my head, whining and cursing his father.

We passed along the south-west wall of Buckingham Palace, the revolving spikes of childhood memory now reinforced by a rack of electrified razor wire. Phil scanned the road for unmarked police cars and the sky for helicopter support, mumbling to himself, imagining the cold

Sheffield click of handcuffs and the screams on the wing in the middle of the night, screams that might soon be his own, simulating Her Majesty's pleasure in the striped shadows of a cell as a villain's hot breath blistered the back of his neck with Greek love. Presently we crossed the river by Vauxhall Bridge beneath the electric eyes of the MI6 building.

'More bloody cameras!' said Phil. 'How many's that make it? I doubt we've been off a monitor for half a minute since Marble Arch.'

I'd never known Phil to be camera-shy before but I shared his unease, picturing our ghost van traversing the various monitors – Marble Arch, Park Lane, Hyde Park Corner, Victoria.

'Why does it always have to happen to me?' Phil complained, as if there was a god in the sky pulling wings off fifty-foot flies.

'It happened to Mark,' I said. 'Keep quiet and let me drive.'

On one of Camberwell's trash-swept arterial boulevards I found a cash dispenser that would take my savings card. It was more of a mug-point than a cash-point. Two teenagers lurked close by in sparkling Nike cross-trainers, harbouring plans to supplement their pocket money, but something about me made them back off and their reaction really disturbed me. What had I become? Would there ever be a way back to the innocent pleasure I'd experienced when the old lady found Phil's hundred pounds? Following my usual and therefore reassuring moment of panic that I'd forgotten my PIN number, I punched in the digits and took a few deep breaths. Whatever else was happening I was glad to be doing something normal (pressing buttons below a small black screen and being slipped cash by a computer), even if it meant halving my net worth.

Phil had grown up in the area and I followed his directions through the back streets, unstitching the skimpy hem of Herne Hill to make a series of turns down roads of somnolent terraced houses that dozed beneath the giant cobweb of telephone lines covering south London. At first I was glad to leave the main drag, but soon the various speed bumps and chicanes of the traffic-calming scheme were driving me barmy. Eventually we came to West Norwood and I made the turn on to the plate-glass desert of the high street with the care of an astronaut executing a space-dock. Deep in a dream state, other drivers were given to random, unsignalled manoeuvres. Tension had driven a six-inch nail down the side of my neck, so I drove slowly, scanning the shop-fronts as they reared up to my right. Phil took the left side of the street and sat up at the windscreen, his face as lined as a street map. The nervous tic in his knee had climbed his trunk to flicker at the side of his mouth. I saw a butcher's shop and braked.

'Is that it?' I asked.

It was halal.

'Course not,' Phil snapped. 'Did you think we'd have to bleed him first? I told you, it's called Vernon's.'

We drove on past discount clothing stores and failing electrical shops. Phil saw it first: Vernon's Family Butchers, the letters spelt out in a bulbous blue serif. When I slowed the van to a stop, the worn brakepads keened.

Inside the shop a strip-light illuminated a window display of empty steel trays bordered by miniature hedgerows of decorative plastic verdure. Phil told me to turn down an alley beside a shuttered jewellery shop and the alleyway was so narrow that I almost missed it. The asphalt road surface had worn away in places to leave lesions through which Victorian cobblestones bubbled. This alley gave on to a mews that ran parallel to the high street, the flip side of the retail coin, a blighted dead-zone used only for deliveries. The left side of the mews was lined with the chipped and battered steel security doors of the shops that faced on to Norwood high street. The right side comprised the wall of a new superstore, its pale bricks bare but for a dozen air-conditioning units caged along its length at ten-yard intervals. Flattened cardboard boxes were stacked in flimsy wire-sided trolleys at the wall's base, alongside tubular roller bins and wooden fork-lift pallets. I drove up the mews in first gear towards the back of the butcher's shop, uncomfortably aware that we'd entered a cul-de-sac. Two smoked and city-aged cars were parked tight up against the superstore wall to permit the passage of delivery vans, one of which blocked our path. Phil was breathing too fast.

'Pull up and switch off the lights,' he said. 'That's Justin's van.'

The van was a dirty white four-wheeled box, fifteen feet high. I parked right behind it, my headlights illuminating the words 'Also available in white', inscribed on the grimy roller door by some black-fingered wag.

'I'll go to the pub and fetch him, yeah?' Phil said. 'You stay in the van.'

I watched Phil pick his way along the side of the old buildings until he disappeared around the corner. The moon outlined a patch of black cloud in silver and I held it together for a minute or so, but then Mark's body got to me and I believed I could detect a whiff of decomposition behind the smell of the paint and the chemicals. Of course I was imagining it – Mark had been dead for only a couple of hours – but I thought I'd scream if I stayed in the van another second. I opened the door and stepped out straight on to a section of expanded polystyrene casing that lay in the roadway. It broke with a loud crack, loose pellets landing in a pool of oil that reflected the moon as a shimmering close-down dot. It was a clear night and the air was so cold that it prickled my nose and throat to breathe it. My breath chuffed from my mouth to freeze in the air and I hugged myself and stamped my feet. When I looked in at Mark through the rear window, there was a faint glow on the pale dustsheet but there was no freehold on life. At best it was a shaky tenancy agreement and I realized then that Sara and I would die along with everyone else. I fought to stave off a rising tide of panic. The whole world pressed in on me, reduced to the size of an anteroom in a morgue.

Phil and I were doing everything wrong.

The shock of Mark's death had thrown my judgement. Justin was crackers. He couldn't be trusted to dispose of a rubber glove, let alone a dead body. I was a berk to have gone along with Phil's hare-brained scheme to get rid of the body. Burke and Hare on rewind. The police would understand. I could explain what had happened. It wasn't too late. I wanted to leave Phil there, sprint to the nearest police station and tell them everything.

There was a noise behind me. Something was moving along the side of Justin's van. I backed into the shadows and tripped, steadying myself against an abandoned supermarket trolley.

'Andy?' Phil called. 'Come and give us a hand. He's gone in round the front.'

I was so happy to hear his voice that I caved in and complied without a murmur. When Phil opened the back of my van, the soles of Mark's shoes stuck out from beneath the dustsheet and I saw that the rubber heels had worn away to expose quarter-moons of pale leather. The heels needed to be replaced – except that they didn't. I was loath to touch the body again, but Phil brushed such tender mercies aside, grabbing the legs to drag Mark's face across the floor of the van. I leaned inside to get a grip on Mark's wrist and he felt appreciably cooler than he had in the flat, and I was pleased about this. When I put an arm round his waist, I found that his stomach was hardening like a bag of cement left out in the rain.

'He feels heavier,' I said.

'Well, he's given up the fags, hasn't he? You always stick on a few pounds,' Phil gasped.

'That's not funny,' I said.

'Nothing's funny,' said Phil.

As we staggered towards the butcher's shop, with Mark's cold curls mopping my cheek at each step, I imagined the corpse becoming heavier and heavier until it broke through the asphalt crust of the mews in a bid for auto-interment. I kept an eye on the windows above the shops but no lights came on and then I saw an L of white light when a back door opened some twenty feet further up the mews.

'That'll be Justin,' Phil said.

Phil pushed the door wide open and the three of us climbed the steps to turn edgewise into a white-tiled cutting room of steel and neon. Phil and I propped Mark against a metal table with a band saw at its far end, allowing him to slide gently to the ground with his head against the band saw's housing. Free of Mark's dead weight, I experienced the strange floating lightness you feel after carrying a child around on your shoulders. There was no sign of Justin, so Phil headed off towards the front of the shop to look for him.

A sharp smell cut through the disinfectant, a sickly sweetness that caught in the back of my throat, and drops of dried blood gleamed on the floor beside an olive-green four-wheeled dumper bin half full of stripped carcasses. I didn't take too close a look, afraid to find leg of human or shoulder of man. It was a vegan's worst nightmare. Vacuum-packed pillows of offal were arranged along the wall beside a loose pile of pig's trotters. On the floor a pool of bloody water twisted the overhead strip-light into a whiplash of white electricity. The words 'Store in a cool dry place' came to mind. In a chill room to the right, separated from the main room by a transparent plastic curtain, I glimpsed eviscerated carcasses of pig, cow, and sheep suspended in rows by their hind legs.

Justin stepped out of a door to my left and closed it on the sound of a flushing toilet.

'How you doing?' he asked.

'Never better,' I lied.

It was a dumb question. How did he think I was doing, heaving a corpse across London in the middle of the night? Justin was wearing white gumboots, jeans and a zipped parka that hid his chin. He was taller than me, around six foot three, and his long biker hair was topped by a wool cap embroidered with a splat logo. We shook hands and my own disappeared into his vast mollusc grip, his boneless fingers scrunching my knuckles together like marbles in a sock.

'My . . . hand,' I gasped.

'Sorry,' he said.

Justin hadn't hurt me intentionally. A long time ago someone had told him that he had a weak handshake and now everybody had to pay the price. Justin wasn't the sharpest tool in the box and he looked as if he was trying to think of something to say. There was no prescribed etiquette for such occasions but it wasn't just that. Something wasn't right with him and I was gripped by a sudden fear that Phil had killed Mark and was about to murder me with Justin's help. That Mark and I would soon be filling gutbomb meat pies in a motorway service station half-way up the M1. Then Justin saw Mark and his jaw hit the floor.

'Who's that?'

Who did he think it was?

'It's the guy,' I said. 'The overdose.'

'You crazy? What you doing bringing him here?'

I didn't understand.

'But Phil arranged it with you,' I said.

Justin's face went yellow-white and he started shaking. I recognized the symptoms of shock and felt the floor tiles fall away beneath me. Justin was terrified – he'd just been boasting. I was in West Norwood with a corpse, a big mouth and a gullible moron, and I had to bite back an urge to head-butt the wall. The three of us made Mark look like a winner. Not a moment too soon, Phil returned from his foray to the front of the shop. I wanted to hit him.

'Hi, Justin,' Phil rasped. 'Well? Let's get on with it.'

'G-get him out of here!' stammered Justin. 'Look, I can't cope with this.'

'Hey, come on,' said Phil, clapping his shoulder. 'What is this? Course you can. It's no big deal.'

'I said we'd talk about it. Shit, you never said you were bringing the bloody body down here!'

Phil's hand smeared the flesh of his cheek.

'I was being discreet, wasn't I? I didn't want to spell it out on the mobile.'

'You're a fucking idiot, Phil,' I said.

And so was I to have trusted him. Mind-bendingly stu-pid. Justin reeled back into a plastic chair. One of the arms was broken and it had been poorly repaired with black woven tape. The tape had budged under pressure to leave deposits of cream-coloured adhesive on the armrest and I thought of the plaster on Mark's finger. The walls began to press in once more.

'I can't do it,' Justin said. 'I tried to say in the pub I just don't want to. I'm serious.'

'For fuck's sake!' Phil groaned. 'You're my bloody cousin!'

'Look, I was just winding you up the other night, all right?'

'Well, you fucking managed it now! What d'you suggest we do, dump him outside in the alley?'

'No! No. But I can't do it. I just can't. I never done it before, see?'

'And? You think I drag dead people across town every fucking day of the week myself? You said it was easy.'

'Why can't you just drop him in a skip or something?' Justin suggested.

'We can't, all right? It's a bit more complicated than that,' Phil said. 'Which is why there's three hundred quid in it for you.'

'It's not enough,' Justin said. 'Not for cutting him up. I'd need at least three grand. To compensate for the psycho-logical trauma, you know.'

'You dozy git!' Phil screeched. 'What is this? We had a deal!'

They were both as crazy as each other and I'd been a blind fool. Sara would be married with kids by the time I got out of prison. I saw myself stepping out through a small door in a big wooden gate, unaccustomed to so much light and space, taking tentative steps with the aid of a Zimmer frame.

'Have you got two and a half grand?' Phil asked me.

'Fuck off,' I said.

I slumped down on the floor to sit opposite Mark. It wasn't the money. Justin simply couldn't bring himself to do it. He didn't have the bottle. I could just picture the creep full of drink, trying to glamorize his duff job with a criminal veneer. Phil turned to him.

'Look, just show me what to do and I'll do it myself, all right? You can go and sit in the van with Andy.'

Phil hit the red button on the band saw, but when the metal hoop whirred into life and out of focus, he leapt back in fright. Acid bile scratched at my tonsils as I imagined the dismemberment.

'So what would you do with the body then, eh?' Phil asked Justin.

The skin tightened around Justin's mouth.

'You really don't want to know,' he said.

'We better start stripping him down, Andy,' Phil said. 'Clothes, any jewellery and stuff. We take all of it away and bury it, all right? I'll cut the clothes off him.'

'No,' I said. 'If you touch him I'm going.'

From a rack of saws and choppers, Phil took a pair of shears with thick curved blades. Justin rushed over to stop him.

'Hang on a sec,' Justin said. 'You're not bloody doing that here!'

Justin pulled Phil away from the body, took a close look at Mark and then he grabbed the head in his big hands and tried to budge it. The head was still bent way over and there was a gruesome crumping sound as Justin attempted to force it back. He ran his fingers over Mark's skull and then he slowly turned to me.

'What did you say happened to him?' he asked.

'He took an overdose,' I said.

'You taking the piss? How'd he do his bloody head in?'

'Come again?' Phil said.

'Fuck off out of it! You topped him, didn't you? Think I'm stupid or what?'

'It's just rigor what's-it, isn't it?' Phil said.

'No, you wanker! Somebody's done his skull in.'

Phil looked devastated, but I didn't believe it. I thought Justin was trying something on, but then he flattened Mark's hair, pointed to an area on the back of the head, and I ran my fingers over a ridge the size of an alp. Surprisingly, it had taken a professional butcher to find it. We hadn't even looked. Mark had been bludgeoned to death and my brain spun backwards like a wagon wheel in a Western. There was some greasy blood on my fingers. I was surprised there wasn't more.

'I want you both out of here,' Justin said. 'Now.'

13

'Out!' Justin snarled at us.

We couldn't move or even speak. Justin pushed Phil against the wall and snatched a long boning knife from a magnetized wall-strip. When Phil started to protest, Justin cut him off, using the point of the knife to describe a loose figure-of-eight in front of his face.

'All right, all right! We'll go!' Phil said.

I could hardly breathe – a passenger on a sinking liner with his face pressed to the cornice of a flooded ballroom. Phil was shouting at me to help him move Mark's body and then the back of Mark's busted head was digging into me and we were retreating into the mews. I was so hyped up that the body felt light and slack as an old pillow from a derelict room. Justin slammed the door on us and I slipped on a wet cobble to stumble into the side of his van. It boomed like a bass bin and Phil swore at me. Mark's body fell and his head hit the ground with a soft eggshell crack. Phil was still swearing at me as we shoved Mark into the van and backed up the mews. I yelled at him to shut up and pulled out of the alley on to Norwood high street.

'What happened, Andy? What happened? Did you get back and find Mark in bed with Sara? Was that it? Pick something up and whack him?'

'I didn't touch him!' I shouted.

'So what the fuck happened? Watch out!'

I swerved to avoid a cyclist.

'Try not to add to the body count.'

Sweat beaded up on my forehead and when I wiped it away the skin felt cold as porcelain.

'Shit, we've moved the fucking body!' Phil said. 'That makes us accessories. We'll have to weigh it down and dump it in the river.'

In my mind I saw Richard's car circling the square, dragging the empty bottle of pills on the end of a length of string.

'We can't dump anything in the river,' I said. 'That's exactly what Richard wants us to do.'

Richard had killed Mark and he'd set us up to boot. I knew it on a cellular level. Richard's control-freak temper, the sight of his car in the square just after Mark's murder . . . It was as clear as a slide show: Richard taking Sara's call, then going round to the flat and throwing a wobbler; Mark hitting his father; a fight; a panicked Richard setting the overdose scene. And two fools buying it.

'Richard?' said Phil.

'Of course. We'd be helping him get away with it. I told you I saw him in the square.'

Phil looked at me with sick, tired eyes, their huge pupils pinpricked with tiny lights that dug into my own like the points of a compass. He gulped in bewilderment.

'You saw a car like his,' he said.

'I saw the number plate. Something JBK. We'll have to go and check, but I'm sure I'm right.'

Phil twitched in the passenger seat, substituting his lower lip for chewing gum.

'Shit, what if it was him?' Phil asked. 'What if he's told the police about us?'

'He probably has by now if he's got any sense. To set us

up. But they won't be looking for us at his place, will they?'

The streetlights sprayed the tarmac with chips of yellow rain. The traffic moved slower north of the river, in fits and starts like a bleeding animal, and the trip to Regent's Park became a water torture in the collective car wash of the rush-evening. All around us drivers buffed up their own worries – bankruptcy, bodged face-lifts. Nothing that couldn't be put right. Not like us. My nerves were shredded and I doubt if my pulse rate dropped below a gallop the whole way to the Bowrings' house. Meanwhile, the blood in Mark's veins was getting stickier in the back of the van. It was one thing for us to have tried to get rid of an overdose, quite another to be covering up a murder. Murder. Mark had been murdered. I tried to get my head round the idea – no, the fact – and kicked myself for buying the staginess of the pill bottle and the whole faked-up scene.

It was eleven p.m. by the time we reached the crescent. There was no sign of the police but lights blazed on the first and second floors of the Bowrings' house as I drove past in second gear. Richard's sports car was parked beyond it and my headlights bounced off the number plate: something JBK.

'Jay bloody Kay,' I said. 'See? I told you it was Richard.'

Phil's Adam's apple yo-yoed up and down to pump some saliva into his mouth but I felt oddly calm, the way I had when Sean bearded me at the station – as stable as a child's gyroscope on a plummeting 747. Now Richard was back in his mansion, while we carted his victim's corpse past his window. We'd played straight into his cupped bloody hands and the van's wiper blades wagged at us in reproof across the rain-swept windscreen.

'What about Sara?' Phil asked. 'If she made the call to

Richard, she can prove he knew where to find Mark. At least it'd be a start.'

There was something in what he said. Somehow we had to get Richard to crack and confess to the police. Sara had known Richard since childhood, so if he had a conscience to prick, she was the person to do it. Phil didn't have her number and he wanted to phone Dean to ask him for it, but any call on Mark's mobile would be traceable so we searched out a phone box and crammed inside to make the call. Phil stabbed in Dean's digits with an unsteady fore-finger, got the engaged tone and redialled twice. I was worried about the call he'd made to Justin from the flat, but there was nothing we could do about it so I kept my mouth shut. A tumbleweed of cassette ribbon blew across the wet pavement, hit a lamppost and made a looping scrawl for the gutter.

A police car came down the street and appeared to slow as it drew level with my van, but fortunately it drove on to ruin someone else's evening. When the operator told Phil that Dean's phone was off the hook, Phil suggested we hole up in his flat in Hammersmith to think things through.

'There's no time for that,' I said. 'We've got to go round to Dean's and wake him up.'

Phil agreed, and before we left the booth I called Jeff's number to see if Sara had left a message on the machine, but there was only a directive from Emma Bowring telling me to repaint a radiator. She complained that I'd scuffed it and her mild pique was a reminder of the kind of everyday cares Phil and I had left far behind. Driving to Shoreditch, my mind scurried like a lab rat in a maze, butting various dead-ends until I parked the van outside Dean's building, choosing a dark space away from the streetlights. We dis-guised the shape of Mark's corpse as best we could, adding a crumpled tarpaulin to the pyre, but I was still worried about leaving the van unattended. With no alarm or valid tax disc, it might as well have had 'Insecuricor' stencilled on its side panels. What if someone stole it?

'Then it's their problem, isn't it?' Phil said. 'They can dig Mark a hole and save us the bother.'

I was panting as I climbed the stairs, my anxiety of the night before jacked to the power of ten, and when Phil pressed the buzzer to Dean's flat I wanted to flee. Phil was about to push the buzzer again when Dean opened the door with a grin that was meant for somebody else. He saw us and it disappeared. The pale, puffy state of his face left little doubt that he'd put another twenty-four sleepless hours on his body clock.

'Hey, Phil and Andy,' he said. 'You all right? I think I achieved a personal best last night. How did you get here?'

'We drove,' said Phil.

'Yeah? Get yourselves a drink and I'll be through in a minute,' he said.

Dean disappeared into a bathroom. What would we say if he asked us about Mark? We hadn't worked out a story and I tried to discuss it with Phil, but he ignored me, pushing on into the living area, where several long-distance party-people were scattered about in the gloom.

The air was ripe with spilt drinks and old smoke, and ashtrays overflowed on to the glass table-top. A girl with a yard of shining black hair lay on a floor cushion, her miniskirt little more than a hem. A candle the size of a five-litre paint tin fried on the floor by the black sofa on which a skinny guy sat, illuminated by a dim rattan floor lamp. It was Neil Cheston, the DJ with the grey hair penned into his pigtails. His very name spoke of an urgent need for restraint, but his face told a different tale, the skin so bleached and the eyes so red that he appeared to exist in an unending bloom of camera flash. When I said hello he raised his head.

'You know Phil Jessup?' I asked him.

Neil looked too whacked out to remember what day it was, let alone a has-been singer, but Phil was still a little miffed.

'Hi,' he said, effecting a complex ritual handshake that left Neil even more baffled.

'Gootomeet you,' Neil mumbled, racking out an inch of abstracted grin.

I figured Neil might know Sara's number, and if I could get it without tipping Dean to the fact that I didn't have it, so much the better. There seemed little chance that Neil could pin down eleven digits in the bouncy castle of his cerebellum but when I asked him for it he drew a Psion organizer from his trouser pocket, swayed unblinking to punch in Sara's name and showed me his little screen with a measure of pride in his achievement. I memorized the number. Fantastic, as Mark used to say. Something was going right at last. I thanked Neil, said goodbye and was ready to drag Phil away from the girl on the floor cushion when Dean emerged from the bathroom.

'So how was the casino?' he asked. 'Mark's a lovely geezer, isn't he? Really open.'

I didn't tell Dean that Mark was at that moment as closed off as you could get.

'Do you know where Mark is?' Dean asked Phil. 'I'm meant to be seeing him with Sara and I tried to call him on his mobile.'

Dean rubbed at his nose and I chewed the inside of my cheek.

'He stayed the night at Andy's place and left around lunch time,' Phil replied.

I was worried Phil would forget what he'd said, so I made a mental note of it. We now had a story to remember and I wondered how many times we'd be called on to recount and embellish it.

'We thought he might be here,' I said. 'That's why we came over.'

Dean grunted and asked Phil where we were headed.

'My place in Hammersmith,' Phil said.

'You couldn't give us a lift to Chelsea, could you? If it's not out of your way?' Dean asked. 'It's just I've got to see someone and I'm not really up to driving.'

Chelsea was more or less on our route, so there was no way to refuse Dean without alerting his suspicions. The demolition crew fired the charges and our chance of a clean getaway toppled like an exploded skyscraper.

'Course,' Phil said. 'No trouble at all.'

Phil's face turned a greener shade of pale. Dean had played him perfectly and our only hope was to steer Dean into the front seat and keep him distracted. If he happened to turn round and see the outline of Mark's body over the back seat, we were going to go to prison.

Following Phil and Dean down the stairs, I felt as powerless as an anarchist with a parking ticket. I was almost hoping that the van had been Taken Without the Owner's Consent, but it was still parked in the shadows so I opened the passenger door for Dean. Phil climbed into the back, Dean took the front seat, and my fingers weren't so much crossed as plaited in my pocket. Luckily for us, Dean's curiosity extended little further than the end of his own nose. He was in an advanced state of refreshment and anxious to boast of his new projects, quite forgetting that he'd told me all about them the previous night. I tried to sound fascinated, but Dean said I seemed nervous and I lied that it was because I was nudging the drink-driving limit. Phil sat forward on the back seat, his head wedged between Dean and me to obscure Dean's view of Mark. We skirted the West End and were driving along the Embankment before Dean wound down his pitch and switched his attention to the subject of Sara and the trip to the casino.

'I've been there a few times with Mark. Cost me a fortune. Actually Mark still owes me a grand from the last time,' he said. 'But we had a real hoot. Did Sara enjoy herself?'

'She seemed to, yes,' I said.

'That's good. That's what she needs. She was a bit stressed last night, I thought. She works so hard. I keep telling her to take it easier.'

'Sound advice,' said Phil.

'Did you go on anywhere afterwards?' Dean asked me.

'No, just back to mine for a bit,' I said.

I could feel him crawling all over me, looking for a way to find out if Sara had stayed the night. Getting nowhere, he tried another tack.

'Didn't you and Sara have a thing together, Andy? When we shot your video?'

'Yes, for two minutes,' I said. 'That was a long time ago.'

There was no way I was going to serve up my feelings for Sara as an emotional smorgasbord.

'It was a nice video, though. Even if I do say so myself,' said Dean. 'Shame the single never really happened.'

'The song was all right. It was your bloody vid if anything,' sneered Phil. 'That bullfight stuff, it was fucking shite. I had death threats from the Animal Liberation Front!'

It was a relief to drop the subject of Mark and Sara, and the three of us argued about the merits of the video all the way down the King's Road until we reached a block of flats near World's End. As soon as Dean's mountaineering trainers hit the pavement I sped away, an animal set free. Phil was laughing.

'Thank fuck he didn't turn round!' he said. 'I thought we were tits up back there.'

We weren't out of the woods yet, more like down a mole-hole in the Black Forest, but things did look up when I called Sara's number from a phone box and her flatmate told me that Sara had gone down to her parents' place in Wiltshire for a few days to finish an essay. Her hippie mother and stepfather were away on holiday and the house was empty. I was cock-a-hoop to know Sara's whereabouts and felt confident I could find the house again because I'd spent one of the happiest weekends of my life there, crunching through the autumn countryside with Sara while she named the different trees for me. And then forgetting all about them in the Jacuzzi.

'Let's go down there now,' I said. 'We've got to get out of London.'

'Yeah? It's almost one o'clock,' Phil said. 'You sure you could find the place in the dark? Safer tomorrow in the daylight.'

We decided to spend the night at Phil's flat and head off first thing in the morning.

14

I turned off the Hammersmith roundabout under the fly-over to pass in front of the Labatt's Apollo. We'd played there once, the four of us arriving in a limousine arranged by the label with little idea that we'd ultimately be footing the bill for such extravagance ourselves. Now the illumi-nated marquee flagged a flagging American singer-song-writer and one of the flyover's support pillars bore an instance of the ubiquitous mid-1990s graffito WHO IS CHRISTIAN GOLDMAN? – a tease campaign that had so far failed to gain its author a recording contract. The painted words would decorate the bridges and underpasses of London and New York for years to come, no longer a ques-tion so much as an existential howl.

Phil lived in a Victorian mansion block sandwiched between the Apollo and the headquarters of Polygram Records UK Ltd, and I parked in a dead-end street behind his building. Remembering how easily he'd broken into the van that afternoon, I double-checked the locks twice before following him round the block. My senses had been rubbed so raw by the drive with Dean that everything was charged with a sharp, almost painful clarity, and as Phil scrabbled for his key I stared at his surname Dymo-taped by a buzzer, the letters pressed out of the blue plastic strip and strained into whiteness. We went inside, stepping over treacherous piles of banana-bright junk mail to pass along a dimly lit shock corridor of kidney-punching bicycle handlebars and shin-snapping pedals before climbing the linoleum stairs.

Phil's front door opened directly into a small living room and the moment I stepped inside bright light flashed in my face, as if I'd wandered into an empty club with a switched-on stroboscope. I was confused and it took me a moment to realize that the light was coming from outside the window, a free show provided by the mainbeams of cars as they sped past on the flyover at eye level a mere twenty feet away. Phil dragged a thin drape across the window to diffuse the pulsing glare and switched on a puny sixty-watt bulb that hung from the centre of the ceiling. The window looked as if it had been stuck for ever, but the flat felt like a refuge and I began to unwind a fraction.

The living room was decorated in international student mode. Even though Phil had been there only a couple of months, so many layers of flattened take-away cartons, carrier bags, crushed cans and yellowed music papers littered the floor that the place cried out for an archaeologist, not a cleaner. Above a brown sway-backed corduroy arm-chair (the armrests squeegeed with a crust of bright shining dirt) hung the same torn Sex Pistols poster that had decorated Phil's various lodgings since his teens. The poster's four nibbled corners were evidence of his hurried departures from temporary accommodation over the years. I imagined four scraps of acid-yellow paper left tacked to the walls of various rented flats and bedsits as souvenirs of his fleeting habitation, the torn triangles converging on a vanishing point with each new departure. If the poster was on the move from the rectangular to the octagonal, the injunction to 'Never mind the bollocks' had gained a new meaning as Phil's plea for clemency in the light of the setbacks he'd suffered over the intervening decades.

Phil passed through a balsa door into the closed-plan kitchenette and attempted to fire up the boiler, feeding match after match into the small hole at its base, and I shivered against a redundant fridge to observe his efforts until the tiny jets whooshed aflame. There was a bottle of Claymore whisky on the draining board and Phil poked around at the base of a wonky pagoda of unwashed crockery for a pair of suitable drinking vessels. He seemed to feel safer in his lair, but all too soon a spasm of nausea convulsed me again.

I found the bathroom and yanked a white nylon light-cord that darkened on its way down to a plastic bell-bottom. An Xpelair fan clacked into life above my head, the beige louvres flocked with the city's own dark lichen. In this musty, windowless room I attempted to vomit without success, running the cold tap and gazing at the glazed splash-plate behind which a wave of mildew broke out of a strip of poorly applied sealant. Spots of dried toothpaste dappled the surface of a mirror from which my face looked back at me as a strange pale mask punctured by a pair of frightened eye-holes. I splashed water on it and even considered using Phil's ancient sprig of a toothbrush on my teeth.

Back in the living room, Phil handed me a dark-blue mug bearing the legend 'Arsenic' in gold. We drank the Claymore and smoked Phil's tobacco, and when we'd burnt all of it up I went to the garage for more, lung cancer being low on my list of concerns. When I returned to the flat, I discovered Phil stooped over an Omnichord, a small portable Japanese keyboard, recording his creative short-comings on a pocket dictaphone that he'd gaffer-taped to the end of the instrument.

'Leave it out,' I said. 'Listen, I think I'll go in to work tomorrow. I want to see the guilt on Richard's face.'

'That's the drink talking. What about the police? No, it's too dangerous.'

We chipped at the Claymore and argued about it till somewhere near three o'clock, when Phil yawned as if he was trying to snap his jaw clean off, revealing some haphazard tin-rich teeth behind the new ones from K-Mart. He zigzagged to his bedroom and I sat there in the strobe-smashed living room, unable to sleep. I thought of Sara at her parents' place, tucked up in the same big bed we'd shared the weekend I'd stayed there. Spooked by the empty house, Sara had snuggled into my arms, her exaggerated fears a prelude to lovemaking. Now she was in the house on her own and I pictured her making notes in the margin of a book, unwilling to turn off the bedside light until the letters began to wriggle on the page, like minnows in spilt milk. I wanted her naked body, but I was slumped in Phil's armchair watching headlight beams sweep across the ceiling as if the building was itself revolving, room spin becoming building spin.

In the morning I woke with a head full of broken toys to see Phil sipping tea by the soot-specked window, frowning as he searched for the hairline crack where his headache ended and the outside world began. It took me a minute to find my glasses on the floor beside the chair. Beyond the double-glazing, cars slowed to a standstill on the flyover, accelerating their drivers' stress levels from nought to sixty in the five seconds it took them to brake into the tail-back. When I sat up, my head pounded with the sullen serial thud of the Claymore. Phil attempted to clear his chest, an effort akin to dredging the La Brea tar pits, and my own respiratory system was tar-papered from all the cigarettes I'd smoked.

'I just can't get it into my head that Mark's dead,' Phil croaked.

'Tell me about it,' I replied. 'We shouldn't have touched a thing, let alone moved him. We've really fucked this up.'

'We had no choice!'

Phil was tense and tetchy and I was sure that he'd already fretted over the situation for a grey hour or so. I slurped lukewarm tea and decided to go to work. If the Bowrings didn't yet suspect my involvement, they soon would if I failed to show up. Besides, I wanted to see what kind of shape Richard was in and to get some time to think away from Phil. When I told him, he was as dubious as he had been the night before. After all, he still believed the police had been at Marylebone Station.

'What if they've tracked you down through Jeff?' he asked.

'That's a bit far-fetched. Anyway, I need to see Richard face to face first. Just to be sure.'

A mobile phone chirped in the pocket of Phil's jacket. Mark's mobile phone. The hair stood on the back of my neck and Phil jerked forward.

'Don't answer it,' I said.

'You think I'm nuts?'

The phone took a message and when Phil played it back, he said it was Dean asking Mark to call him. I replayed it for myself and thought Dean sounded anxious.

'There's no message from Richard. You'd think he'd have called the mobile by now,' Phil said. 'To find out if Mark was safe.'

It hadn't crossed my mind, but Phil was right: Richard hadn't called because he knew his son was dead. I felt nauseous and my sore lungs crackled like sweet paper. Worse, my T-shirt stank of Mark's pungent hair oil. I took it off and threw it into a corner, but the smell stayed with me and I had a horror that it would just keep getting stronger until I choked on it. When I asked Phil for a replacement, I discovered that his bedroom stood little chance of a pictorial feature in one of Emma's interior-design magazines. Two piles of clothes lay on the floor and, as Phil bent to sift through one of them, I saw his old stage clothes hanging preserved in plastic zip-wrappers on a chrome rail. There was dust along the tops of the shoulders and through the dulled plastic I made out the fringes of the buckskin jacket that he'd bought in Paris. Cracked trainers were perched outside on the window-ledge, a pair of pigeon-repellents training for nothing at all.

'This pile's sort of clean,' Phil said, sniffing tentatively at the sleeve of a grey sweat-shirt.

'What do you mean, clean?' I said. 'I can feel the heat coming off it.'

The thought of decomposition made me think of Mark's body outside in the cold van.

'Just the thing,' said Phil, holding up a pink T-shirt.

It was barely big enough to fit me and I reckoned it was probably a trophy from some teenybopper conquest, but I squeezed into it and got ready to go. There wasn't much more to do at the Bowrings' and I told Phil that I'd be back at midday, promising that we'd leave for Wiltshire just as soon as I returned. Sensing my determination, Phil gave up and slumped back in the armchair to stare at the flyover, and the T-shirt cut into my armpits as I swung my arms on my way down the stairs.

The air felt warmer outside but the sky was the colour of a switched-off neon tube. I went to check on the van and one glimpse of Mark's shrouded corpse set my heart bumping. The shape of the body was just discernible beneath the tarpaulin, so I opened the back door and climbed inside to disguise it some more. I was prepared for the reek of decay but the air in the van was thick with the smell of paint and chemicals as I lifted the sheet to catch an unhappy snap of Mark. I placed some more paint tins and a small stepladder alongside his body. When I accidentally brushed his arm with my hand, I sensed it was horribly cold beneath the fabric. Grabbing my tool-bag, I got out of there in a hurry, bought a pay-and-display ticket for four hours' parking time, thumbed its adhesive backing to the windscreen and relocked the van.

A grimy church abutted the far side of the flyover's cantilevered span and it even crossed my mind to go inside and pray for Mark's soul. A real waste of time. Paging a notional deity while a thousand cars sped overhead would have been like trying to fly a paper dart through an avalanche. I guess one consolation for the vicar was the lack of roofing bills, since a new layer of lead would be laid down every year by the traffic passing overhead. Entering the wraparound mind-warp of Hammersmith Broadway, I crossed at the traffic lights in front of a lorry-load of prisoners who'd been sunglassed and cubicled by Group 4, and I was sobered by the thought that I'd be sharing the same diminished view and improving shareholder return soon enough if I wasn't careful. On the far side of the roundabout two kids no more than eight years old were running through the moving traffic to clean windscreens for chump change, and a police car drove past them without stopping.

On the Hammersmith and City Line train I succumbed to the crippling sense of isolation that accompanies the purchase of an underground ticket and took a long, hard look at things. Although I'd always thought of myself as a good person, I couldn't square this with my theft of the stamps and the drive to West Norwood. My moral values seemed about as secure as the Mir space station and I chased the thoughts that clattered through my mind. If we were arrested, Phil had made the calls. I wouldn't be charged as an accomplice to the extortion, just for failure to notify. No real need to worry on that score.

Yet I did worry, because no amount of self-deceptive steam could quite iron out my wrinkle of wrongdoing. The faces of the other passengers scratched over me like little pads of suspicion, but the thought of the stamps was a far worse torment. However noble my intentions had been at the time, I'd not returned the stamps and now Mark was dead. It didn't look good, it looked like five years at least, and I berated myself for not having taken the stamps from the van and hidden them. But where? The stations shot by and the advertisements on the platforms bulged with muscle-wadded male torsos seemingly designed to point up the shortcomings of ectomorphs like myself. I disembarked at Baker Street and walked past the convex lens of Sherlock Holmes's magnifying glass in a blown-up Victorian ink drawing that decorated the wall-tiles. A busker was singing that he didn't want to hurt us, that he didn't want to make us cry and that he was swallowing his pain. Swallow mine, I thought. Swallow mine.

I caught another train to Regent's Park and on a quiet road near the Bowrings' crescent I came upon an old man in a herringbone overcoat standing in the middle of the pavement. He was doubled up and mumbling to himself, a hand to the far side of his face, apparently gripped with an unspeakable grief. I felt a surge of empathy. The man's enormous ear was still growing even as his bones were shrinking, and I was on the point of asking if I could help in any way when I saw that he was speaking to someone on a mobile phone.

I pressed on across the slabs of York stone, casting no more than a momentary smudge of shadow, and turned on to the crescent. When I saw the Bowrings' house my bravado began to ebb and I slowed my pace. There was no sign of the police, but terror rose in my throat as I walked up to the front door and pressed the bell. I was doing something crazy, not just reckless but actively self-destructive. What if the police really were looking for me? I was about to turn heel when Richard Bowring opened the door.

I was startled but no more so than Richard. Straight away I saw fear in his bug-eyes. Fear and what I took to be guilt. He looked so haggard, it was obvious he hadn't slept, and he'd even omitted to grease his hair. We stood there looking at each other, unsure.

'I thought you'd finished,' he said.

'Just the shelves left really and a bit of touching up,' I replied. 'Then I'll be out of your hair.'

Unruly tufts of it flapped over his ears and he ran a hand over them in search of some self-possession. Then he opened his mouth to say something else but thought better of it and pushed past me into the street. Richard had lost his silvery sheen of wealth and power. There was no sign of Ildikó, so I went to the dining room and tried to calm down as I pulled on my paint-crusted whites over my paint-crusted jeans. The house was extraordinarily quiet for London. This was the kind of silence you buy, silence that really is golden. Silence that costs an arm and a leg, or in this case perhaps a whole body. The dustsheets were laid out just as I'd left them the previous afternoon and it was hard to believe that I'd used one just like them as an improvised shroud for Richard's son. I thought of Mark's corpse in my van, along with the stamps.

The stamps.

The pigskin folder revolved on a turntable in my mind. I hadn't even told Phil I had them. What was I to do? Return them anonymously? Throw them away? I saw the police getting lucky raking a waste dump and a zealous white-coated dweeb tweezering a speck of Farrow and Ball Pigeon White from one of the album's leaves. Struggling to plug a pumping fountain of paranoia, I started to put another coat on the shelves, working my way along a scaffold plank perched on trestles. The door opened behind me and Emma Bowring stood there wearing a black leotard with a rollneck and a pair of leggings. She'd been working out in her little gym upstairs and her yellow hair culminated in wet avian points.

'Morning, Andy,' she said. 'Is everything all right?'

Emma was breathing hard from her exertions and she looked anxious. Did she know about Mark's death?

'Never better. Um, any news of Mark?'

She moved lazily towards me, a shallow woman wading through shallow water.

'He was behind the whole thing,' she said. 'Someone phoned Richard and told him. A girl.'

My throat tightened. It was no more than I'd suspected, but it still hurt to have it confirmed that Sara had called Richard even though Mark had given her reason to believe I was involved.

'So Mark's safe then?' I asked.

'Well, we don't know, do we? The girl said Mark was in some flat in Kilburn, but there was no answer when

Richard sent the police round there. Maybe the call was a hoax.'

I turned to slap some paint on to the shelves so that Emma couldn't read my face. Richard's remarkable sang froid had left me speechless: he'd killed his son, set us up and then called the police. Phil had been right about Richard's resourcefulness. If we'd gone to the police ourselves we'd be facing a light-year apiece. Luckily for me, the phone rang and Emma went to answer it, and I heard her tell the caller that Richard was at the office but that he'd be in the country later. She gave the number of Foxton Hall. When she hung up, I expected her to go upstairs, but instead she came back into the dining room. She seemed tense and I asked her what the police had said.

'There's not a lot they can do,' she said. 'Mark's meant to be an adult and the stamps do legally belong to him. I keep telling Richard he's probably sold them and gone abroad for a holiday.'

The word 'stamps' hit a nerve and drilled right into it.

'What stamps?' I asked, not quickly enough.

It was the first time she'd mentioned the stamps in my hearing and I suspected it was some kind of trick. I was six feet up in the air and the plank turned into a high-wire.

'The stamp collection Mark had as a child,' she said. 'Actually we're not sure, but we think it might be worth as much as twenty thousand.'

She lit a Silk Cut.

'Richard's smoking again,' she said. 'He tried to stick to those little cigars, but what d'you expect? It's not just this thing with Mark. He's got a big presentation at Foxton the day after tomorrow and it's giving him ulcers. A hundred people are coming down from London.'

'Oh yes? What's all that about?'

'He wants to turn the main house into a health club. It costs a bomb to run and we're pretty much broke.'

I was stunned.

'You've got to be kidding. What about this place?'

'The lease runs out in a few years. That's why he's so stroppy about the redecoration. Now he's gone into partnership with a group of Malaysians over this health-club thing. If it works out we'll be OK. If not, who knows?'

If it didn't work out I reckoned it was eight to five on that she'd leave him within the year.

'Money isn't everything,' I said.

I'd been rich for a couple of years, the most anguished years of my life.

'I mean, look at Mark,' I said. 'He's still got his fair share of problems, hasn't he?'

She blew smoke at me.

'Mark's never been quite right in the head and now he's completely out of control,' she said. 'Dr Leffler says he lives in a world of make-believe. I almost feel sorry for him. He came over to dinner here the other week and accused Richard of stealing from the trust. In front of our guests. Richard had to cut Mark's allowance to try and get him back into the clinic. Have you done the radiator?'

I hadn't given it a thought.

'Really, Andy. A dazzling inattention to detail.'

I asked her to refill my paint tray from the five-litre tin on the floor and she slithered across the room, treating me to a pelvic floor show as she bent over.

'That's enough paint,' I said.

When she handed it up to me, I knocked the tray against the shelves and a cupful of paint splashed over my whites.

'Shit!'

'How sweet,' she said. 'I think you're actually blushing.'

Emma went to fetch a roll of paper towels from the kitchen and I climbed down the stepladder, tenting the crotch of my whites so as not to drip the puddle of paint. I stood there feeling breakable until Emma returned.

'You'd better do it yourself,' she said.

When I dabbed at my groin, it only made matters worse and wetness seeped through the material into my jeans.

'Why do you always listen to classical music?' Emma asked.

Ravel's Bolero was playing on Classic FM.

'I guess I like it,' I said.

'Were you ever in a band?' she asked.

The needle on my paranoia meter swept through the red and went right off the gauge.

'Er, why do you ask?'

'You said you used to be a musician, remember? And you don't really look the orchestra type.'

'Yes, well, I was in Overload. You probably never heard of us.'

She gulped and pushed some loose hairs behind her ear. I could tell it came as a real surprise to her. It was the first time I'd seen her at a loss for words.

'Are you all right?' I asked. 'We weren't that bad, were we?'

'No. No, not at all. Actually I think I've still got the CD,' she said.

Emma left the room and ran upstairs with hysterical vitality.

Three minutes later she came back with the *Luxury Amnesia* CD.

'See? You had that song. It was catchy.'

'Like a cold. You get over it.'

She struggled to find the notes in her thin contralto and made a real pig's ear of it.

'God, you must be proud,' she said. 'At least you made a mark.'

'Maybe a scratch.'

'Why don't you take off your dungarees?' she asked.

I was still holding them out in the vain hope that they'd dry quicker.

'I'll give you a hand,' she said.

Emma knelt in front of me and I swallowed as she rolled the whites carefully down my legs, taking care not to get paint on her fingers, staring at my crotch. If Emma was thinking about gratifying a groupie impulse, she was three years too late. Flushed with embarrassment and a kind of anger, I stepped out of the whites. She threw them on a dustsheet and then she looked up at me.

'The singer was gorgeous. Are you still friends?' she asked.

I had a stomach-dropping sense that Emma knew everything and that she was just taking her time backing me into a corner. Cats 'play' with mice before killing them only because the release of adrenalin renders their flesh more tender.

'We lost touch. Phil went to America.'

'Really?' she said.

'Ages ago.'

'You're so tense, Andy. Let me give your neck a rub . . . There. God, your muscles are so knotted up!'

I felt dizzy. I thought she was just teasing me and that any second she would turn around and walk out of the room, leaving me standing there like a fool. Instead she put a hand on my cock and squeezed it almost mechanically, gauging her own sex appeal as if it was the tyre pressure on her car.

'Hang on,' I said. 'We can't –'

But it didn't sound like my voice at all. It sounded as though it was coming from a ventriloquist a long way off. Emma kept on squeezing me until I didn't care if the ventriloquist was strangled to death.

'Of course we can,' she said. 'Kiss me.'

It's bad, but there's no getting around the fact that I fucked Emma Bowring the day after I decided I wanted to spend the rest of my life with Sara. I could say I was terrified that Emma would connect me to Mark's disappearance. I could say I thought it would give me some psychological advantage over her if we had sex and that she'd stop pressing me about Phil. I could say that I was out of my mind at the time and that would all be true. But it's also true that when Emma put her small tongue in my mouth I was thrilled. Her lips were thinner than Sara's and I remember it feeling strange. Then Emma unpopped the studs on her leotard and pulled it up over her left breast and I saw the bump of her nipple through the white material of her sports bra. I made a choking sound and felt a pulse in my cock as Emma pulled her tit free, cupping it with her hand and squeezing it. Despite myself, I wanted to suck her nipple. From her wry smile, I saw that Emma was still totally in control.

She clawed at my underpants with her varnished nails until my cock sprang free, a springy mustard-pot surprise, and she pulled at it with no pretence at finesse. I lifted her up and she wrapped her legs round my waist, pressing herself against me. I tottered six or seven paces over to the table with my jeans around my ankles. We nearly didn't make it, but I just managed to perch her on the edge of the table before we collapsed. Emma threw herself back on the table-top and peeled off her leggings.

'What are you waiting for, Andy? Permission?'

I put my cock inside her and she hooked her legs behind me and drew me towards her. I began to fuck her. She held me still with her legs.

'You can't come inside me,' she said.

Her belly button was deep as the knotted mouth of a balloon.

'OK,' I said.

'Promise?'

I nodded and she pushed me away with her legs. She turned round to lie face down on the dining table, gripping its edge. As I crouched down to fuck her from behind I asked myself what the fuck I was doing.

'Pull my hair,' she moaned.

Puzzled, I did as she asked, tugging at her thick locks with each thrust. She asked me to pull it harder. I looked out of the window at a grey slice of London and then I looked down at my cock going in and out of Emma, feeling like a tired acrobat. There was a patch of white at her coccyx and I worked out that it must have been where contact with a sunbed's surface had prevented the UV rays from working. Emma had been artificially boosting the tan she'd picked up in Bermuda, because the rest of her body was a uniform caramel. I began to fuck her faster and soon I felt a wetness over my thighs. I thought she'd peed herself for a second but it didn't feel like pee. It was thicker, more glutinous.

'God! Don't stop!' she cried. 'It's always like that.'

It was like a fountain had gone off down there and it spurred me on, a salmon leaping upstream. Then she clutched my hip, digging her nails in hard. I cried out in pain and she pushed me back, out of her.

'Did any go on my leotard?' she asked over her shoulder. 'Get the kitchen roll, would you?'

Nonplussed, I shook my head. She felt up her back for a ribbon of sperm that wasn't there.

'I didn't come,' I said.

I felt as awkward as a piece of exercise machinery. There was a sound in the hall and Emma stepped swiftly into her leggings. I pulled up my jeans, zipping them just before Ildikó appeared in her overcoat to ask Emma if she wanted anything from the shops. Emma shook her head, allowing herself a little sigh as Ildikó left the house.

'That was lucky!' I said. 'Christ, a minute earlier –'

'Relax. I'd have heard her.'

Emma sat on the dining table, swinging her legs. She lit a Silk Cut with a slim throwaway lighter and I bummed one off her.

'I didn't think you smoked,' she said.

'Only on special occasions.'

Emma circumflexed an eyebrow as if to say she didn't put too high a value on either abstinence or my sexual performance. Then the phone rang and she raced upstairs to take it on another extension. I fixed the mark on the radiator, feeling sick and empty inside, and tried to tell myself that the sex didn't matter because I wasn't really going out with Sara. And I hadn't come, so in Clinton-speak there was nothing amiss. But it did matter and even though I'd seen what I took to be evidence of guilt on Richard's face, I was even more rattled than I had been before I'd arrived. When Emma came back downstairs twenty minutes later, fully dressed with blow-dried hair, she seemed like a different person. When I told her that I'd have to return to pick my stuff up because the van had a flat battery, she didn't mind a bit.

'Come back and finish off tomorrow if you like,' she

said. 'It'll give me a chance to go to the bank. I'll pay you then.'

It was perplexing. Earlier she'd needed something from me, but now she just wanted me out of her house and there was nothing in her behaviour to suggest that we'd had sex half an hour earlier. If it hadn't been for little details like the white patch at her coccyx, I might almost have dreamt the whole thing.

'You must think me strange,' she said. 'It's just that Richard and I hardly touch each other any more. He says it's because of the stress he's under with his business, but it's not just him. I have a problem with intimacy. My father never touched me after I reached puberty. He couldn't cope with my sexuality. And that's probably why I married an older man . . .'

She kept on in this vein until it started to sound as if such insights had followed the transference of a substantial sum from Richard's bank account to that of a shrink. After five minutes of confessional I began to think she'd fucked me only so she'd have someone to talk to with a cheaper hourly rate.

'It's all right,' I said when she paused for breath. 'As far as I'm concerned it never happened.'

'Promise?'

I nodded and she seemed to relax a bit. Then I packed my stuff away and found myself being reeled back to Hammersmith through the underground system by the van's quiet cargo.

15

In a flat on the ground floor of Phil's building a man in a vest yawned and scratched himself in the cold glow of lunch-time television, happily unaware of the dead body chilling fifty feet from his window. I bought another parking voucher and when I opened the van, the briefest glimpse of Mark's body stripped away the morning and magnified the feeling of raw emptiness I'd been fighting against. Phil buzzed me up and met me on his landing, glancing up and down the corridor like a tennis fan on fast forward. I sensed a bad case of cabin fever.

'What took you so long? I thought you'd bloody been arrested!'

He made me describe the scene at Regent's Park and was delighted that Richard had looked so shaky. I told Phil everything except for the sex with Emma, partly because I felt guilty and partly because I could all too easily see him telling Sara about it. He paced his tiny sitting room as I answered his questions.

'We'll get Sara and go over to Richard's,' he said. 'Sounds like he's ready to crack.'

I shrugged. As a strategy, it felt hopelessly loose and optimistic.

'If we tell Sara, she'll try to make us go to the police,' I said. 'If she doesn't call them herself, that is.'

'She won't do that. She's into you!'

'We haven't seen each other in years and then we spend a night together, that's all. If I show up at her stepdad's with Mark's dead body, she'll go to the police. I would.'

'Course she won't! She was there when we planned it, remember? You just have to explain the way it's all happened.'

Phil cast any doubts he may have had into a sports bag, but when he shored up his enthusiasm by humming an old Police tune, Dr Freud snipped a notch in his cigar at the unconscious association. I was dreading the drive down to the country. A male penguin finds a perfect pebble for his mate and rolls it to her feet, but what would I be bringing Sara? The corpse of her childhood friend. The thought of the off-white non-Bermuda Triangle at the base of Emma's spine made me feel faint. I hadn't eaten anything in twenty-four hours, so I searched out a tin of baked beans in the kitchenette and rummaged in a bag of white bread for some slices that weren't turning into penicillin. As I stirred the beans on the cooker, I watched the tip of the wooden spoon describe a sequence of zeros on the bottom of the pan. The future was orange.

In the sitting room Phil gorged on the pabulum of MTV with the sound turned low, splicing in his own vocal track to slag off each and every act as derivative, oblivious to the fact that we'd ripped off just about everything we'd ever written. I doled him two doleful dollops of sugary beans in a cracked cereal bowl and killed pop music's Sky TV burial over his objections. Phil was anxious to leave and barely touched his food. When I'd finished eating (or subsisting), we went down to the van and I had to force myself to unlock the door. There was a bad smell inside and I wound the window down despite the cold as we passed beneath the flyover and turned off the roundabout heading west. I couldn't shake off my misgivings.

'Just think of this as an undertaker's van,' Phil suggested. 'You see them the whole time. Those little vans with Private Ambulance written on them? They're whizzing dead bodies all over the place. No different to us.'

'Except for some pesky paperwork. Listen, Phil. I can't face telling Sara about this. I want to keep her out of it.'

'I don't see how we can, old man. But don't worry. You'll find the right way to do it.'

Phil tried to pull a sympathetic face, but I'd seen better on Australian soaps. As he lit another cigarette with the stub of its predecessor, I felt for the edge of the album beneath my seat, hoping I'd get a chance to hide it in the country somewhere. As we headed out of London on the motorway, the sun broke through a slit in the clouds to light up a glass-fronted office block that glittered gold against a grey sky. It caught my eye and Phil flipped out.

'Keep half an eye on the road, will you? You missed that truck by a fucking millimetre.'

To try and relax, he started playing his Omnichord and singing into his dictaphone. I begged him to shut up and he looked hurt, but at least he put the instrument back in his sports bag.

'You see all these tyre marks?' he asked.

There were black rubber marks on the pale stretch of road, hatched where anti-lock brake systems had kicked in and out.

'See how they sort of veer off into the crash barrier? Well, there's always a fresh bit, isn't there? Where the mangled section's been replaced. Makes you wonder what happened to the car. If you get my drift.'

We drove in silence, wrestling with our own thoughts and fears. Phil took the remains of the Claymore from his sports bag and glugged the last few units, while I tried to think of some way out of the mess without involving Sara. If the very worst came to the very, very worst, I figured that Phil and I could always bury the body in a wood and stick to our story that Mark had left Jeff's at lunch time. But that would let Richard off the hook and I knew I could never live with the guilt.

The distance between the exits stretched until we finally left the motorway at Hungerford to enter the world of the mini-roundabout. Hardly countryside, it was really a prosperous suburb spread thin – SW197. Vehicular pretension increased sharply and we looped through another daisy chain of mini-roundabouts to circle the town. It was a safe bet that this area had returned a Tory at the last election, and I was worried we'd be mistaken for New Age travellers and wind up on one of the preserved gibbets that I'd seen on the walks I'd taken with Sara.

'Speed up,' Phil said.

Drawing on my dwindling reserves of patience, I explained that you tend to drive cautiously with a dead body on board, the corpse having considerably more charge than a rubber skeleton dangling from the rear-view mirror.

'Try and enjoy the view, can't you? Look at the trees,' I said.

'I can count the fucking leaves, the speed you're going.'

Phil started playing another little tune on his keyboard and I was about to tell him to can it when, to my surprise, it began to grow on me. Like something fungal. I felt fairly sure that I'd be able to recall the way to the house and when we reached the landmark statue of King Alfred in the centre of Pewsey, I took the second road out of the town. After a mile I turned left at the end of a flint wall and followed a narrow winding lane the width of a single vehicle, bordered by high hedges. We passed a large cottage thatched with grey straw, the zigzag patterning at the top reminding Phil of an intricate hip-hop haircut. The light was dropping by the minute and I was becoming anxious that I'd taken the wrong turn. Then I recognized the two tall trees on the hill behind Sara's parents' place and the house itself appeared beyond a five-bar gate that filled a break in the hedge.

'This is it,' I said.

'You're going to have to tell her,' Phil said.

'I'll try.'

Set some way back from the lane, the modern two-storey house had a flat roof and an abandoned air, less detached than disconnected. The ground floor was rendered in concrete and the upper floor wrapped in weathered grey clapboard. There was no car to be seen but the doors were closed on a garage. I looked for somewhere to park the van out of sight of the road and found a track a little further up the lane. The track ran along the edge of a wood and I steered us up the twin tyre-cropped channels that bordered a Mohican strip of grass. I killed the engine, closed the door as quietly as possible and took a quick look at Mark's body to make sure that it hadn't budged from the turns. Phil and I then headed down the slight incline towards the house across a bumpy lawn. There were no lights in the windows and no curlicues of smoke from the chimney stack. A row of tall conifers stood behind the house. The front door had a knocker in the form of a dolphin taking a nose-dive and I struck it, calling Sara's name. There was no reply.

The garage door opened with a shriek of metal and I

switched on the light. There was only one car in there, an ancient Chrysler with flat tyres and bodywork freckled with rust. In some places the metal was as holed and brittle as brandy snap. Bright-green mould had climbed up the side of an old sofa to obscure the William Morris fabric, nature reclaiming its representation, and a windsurf board with an unwrapped sail lay behind the car. Phil and I headed round to the back door of the house, and when I brushed the wall I dislodged flakes of white paint from the concrete with my fingertips. The place was gloomier and more run-down than I remembered it, but then the house might have said much the same of me. I banged on the back door and called out to Sara. It was beginning to look as if she wasn't there and I felt a sweet-sour mix of relief and disappointment.

'It doesn't matter,' said Phil. 'We can leave Mark here while we take a look at Richard's place.'

'Er, yes. All right. Where do you want to put him?'

'Behind that windsurf board in the garage,' said Phil. 'Did you see how dusty it is? Nobody's used it in years.'

It was getting quite dark and we'd have to carry Mark's body only a few feet from the van, so I backed it up to the garage. The ground was frozen, so it was lucky we weren't planning to bury Mark. Yet. The body had stiffened up and seemed to weigh less, as if Mark had suffered at the hands of a frugal taxidermist. One of his shoes came off and I chucked it in the back of the van. Once we were inside the garage, I saw that his fingers and ears were tinged with blue and I mentioned this to Phil.

'Well, he was never the picture of health, was he?' Phil said. 'Not a bad drummer, though. Did I ever tell you that?'

We laid Mark out behind the board and pulled the bright sail over him. The garage door shut with a satisfying clunk that promised more 'closure' than it delivered and I reparked the van on the track, feeling a terrible sadness in the cold country air as we plodded back across grass stiffer than carpet tile.

'What's that?'

Phil pointed to a dim stamp-sized square of light that glowed through a gap in the conifer trees behind the house. It was a window and I panicked until I remembered Sara showing me an old barn that her stepdad had converted into a recording studio. He was a recording engineer and I chiefly remembered him for the embroidered waistcoat that he'd worn the one time I'd met him. My heart bumped – I was sure Sara was in there.

'You wait in the van,' I said. 'I'll do better talking to her alone.'

As I passed through the conifers my head banged into a cluster of steel wind-chimes hanging from the branch of a tree, jangling my nerves some more. The barn door opened on a dark space full of pre-digital junk from the 1980s: clapped-out synthesizers; amplifiers; an Atari keyboard and speakers furred with dust. The only light came from the control room, a glassed-in cubicle set against the far wall. Sara was in there working at a PC with her hair tied up and the sight of her knocked the breath out of me. I called out but she couldn't hear because the control room was soundproofed. When I opened the door, Sara turned with a jolt, her eyes softening when she saw me.

'Andy! What are you doing here? Jesus, you scared me!'

I went and kissed her, and her skin was soft and warm.

'I only meant to surprise you.'

'Well, you managed that!' she said, laughing off the shock. 'How did you find out where I was?'

'Your flatmate told me.'

'So you just drove straight down? I thought you'd play a little harder to get.'

'I wanted to see you. Is that so bad?'

'No. No, I suppose not. Why do you look so frightened?'

Taking my fear for fear of rejection, Sara hugged me and we kissed. My body stiffened as I recalled Emma's dry parrot tongue. I was despicable.

The bright honeycomb of a gas heater blazed like a miniature purgatory in the corner of the booth.

'Are you all right, Andy? You look tired.'

'Oh, it's just the drive. How did you get down here?'

'The coach and then a taxi. It's a hassle but I've got a load of work to do and I was going crazy in London. I needed to slow down. I've been all over the place since the break-up with Dario. Then there was Dean and I just don't want to make another mistake. I've been thinking maybe I should spend some time on my own. Before I get into another relationship.'

'I tried that and it stinks. You've got to take a risk.'

'I don't want you to get hurt, that's all.'

I felt bad, knowing full well that the presence of Mark's corpse in her stepdad's garage would do considerably more than hurt her. Then Phil's face appeared out of the murk beyond the double glazing like some white thing swimming up to a bathyscaph window. Sara's expression dropped twenty degrees and the spell was broken. I was furious with Phil for not staying in the van.

'What's he doing here?' Sara asked me.

Phil came into the booth, flashing his cheap teeth.

'Hi, Sara. How's the essay coming along?' he asked.

He came across phonier than Piltdown Man.

'You know this fucking creep called up Mark's dad and asked for the stamps?' she said to me.

I gulped, taken aback by the force of her anger.

'Oh, God, Andy. You're not involved in this, are you?' she asked.

'Up to a point,' I said. 'Phil was in the van when I left work, so I gave him a lift to the station.'

'I don't believe it!' she groaned. 'I thought Mark was lying.'

The gas heater had dried out the air in the control room. Phil fooled with the faders on the enormous unplugged mixing desk, adjusting the levels for a session that would never happen. Sara turned on him.

'You're a nasty piece of work! You were going to rip Mark off, weren't you?'

'Keep your hair on,' Phil said.

'You can't just go around taking things from other people!' Sara yelled. 'Didn't your mother tell you that?'

'It'd all be all right if you hadn't put your oar in,' Phil said. 'We didn't even get the bloody stamps!'

'Where's Mark?' Sara asked me.

My heart rapped against my ribs as if it wanted to be let out of my body.

'Well?'

The moment stretched and sweat bubble-wrapped my brow. Sara blew her fringe from her eyes.

'He's disappeared,' I mumbled.

'What d'you mean, disappeared?'

'When I got back to the flat he'd gone.'

It was the first serious lie I'd ever told her. My knees buckled but Phil stepped in on the offensive.

'Wind your neck in, all right? Mark took off because you called Richard,' he said. 'And you gave him Jeff's address, didn't you?'

Phil was grinding his teeth and Sara squared up to him.

'Yeah, of course I did, you wanker! I was worried about Mark! And I didn't want you dragging Andy into it.'

'You're bloody involved yourself, the way I see it!' he said. 'You were there when Andy had the idea!'

'Phil, why don't you let me talk to Sara alone for a minute?' I said.

He huffed and puffed but he left the barn, hoping that I'd break the news to her. When I tried to take Sara's hand, she pulled away.

'I'm sorry,' I said. 'This is all my fault.'

'It's not your fault. It's bloody Phil's! You've just been stupid. Like sticking your hand in the bloody waste disposal and switching it on, stupid.'

'I had no choice. I had to help him.'

'Oh, please. When are you going to grow up?'

'But he's in a real state. Mark's gone missing and if anything's happened to him and someone finds out about the phone calls –'

'I can see all that, but Phil deserves everything he's got coming, the little shit. He's a bloody waste of carbon.'

If she only knew, she'd think the same of me. Sara caught the despair on my face and took it for contrition.

'It's all right. I'll cool down in a minute,' she said. 'I mean, Phil didn't actually steal the stamps. And I am glad you're here. Honest.'

She kissed me again, but I felt like a cheat.

'Mark'll show up, you'll see,' she said. 'He was always running off as a kid. Let's go over to the house. I'll even try and be civil to Phil if it'll make you feel better.'

Phil stood shivering by the back door with a crippled smile and Sara led us both inside. The house was so cold that I understood why Sara had been working in the sound booth. The cranky central heating took a day or so to burn off the chill and she went upstairs to check on the hot water tank.

'Did you tell her?' Phil asked.

'How the fuck could I? You saw how pissed off she is about the calls.'

'You've got to tell her, Andy. You've got to.'

What I had to do was to get away from the sound of his voice before I smacked him in the face, so I went into a living room with a modern fireplace and stale air. The walls had been rag-rolled red with a slapdash abattoir abandon, a DIY job worthy of the Manson family. Inside I was a mess, torn up with rage and self-loathing. Sara was right. If Phil hadn't made the calls, none of this would have happened. But I also knew I'd played a full part in the unfolding calamity of the last twenty-four hours. A moose's head hung on the wall and the room temperature was so low that it looked as if the animal had broken through from the steppe, got stuck and frozen to death. A brightly coloured poster of an elephant-nosed Hindu god was framed opposite the moose, its angry eyes and blue skin suggesting that it was finding the Wiltshire winter far from congenial. An unzipped sleeping bag lay on one of the sofas like the skin of a nylon animal. On the mantelpiece a poorly crafted but no doubt serviceable hookah stood beside a Buddha with a burnt-out joss stick skewered into the pot of his belly. Phil wandered through and sat on a chair in the shape of a giant baseball mitt. I was still angry with him and he had sense enough to keep quiet for once. Then we heard Sara coming back downstairs.

'Be nice,' I told him. 'And don't make any mistakes.'

Sara came into the room wearing an extra jumper.

'It's so cold!' she said, forcing a smile for Phil. 'Why

don't you make a fire? Andy and I'll sort out the tea.'

She led me through to the kitchen, where a steel tap dripped into the sink. Having failed to tempt a rat, a crust of bread lay curled beside a knife on the breadboard, and the walk-in American refrigerator contained so many mouldering perishables that it was due a visit from the UN weapons inspectorate. Sara and I had cooked a meal together in this kitchen, flicking tea towels at each other's naked bodies on a summer night, but now when she hugged me it felt wrong. I was an impostor and I didn't deserve her.

'Why the long face? I told you I'm happy you're here,' she said.

'Sara, I –'

'What?'

'Nothing,' I said, and tried to smile.

Sara made a pot of tea and I carried the tray through to the living room, where Phil had built a fire with some cobwebbed logs and last year's papers, and when he lit it Cherie Blair's cowed smile went up in flames. The social putty of the English tea ceremony served to smooth over the differences between Sara and Phil, but the body in the garage was throwing the collective compass off magnetic north. I was half expecting the tea to pour from the spout and miss the cup by an inch or two, and then the phone rang.

16

'It's probably Mum,' Sara said, picking up the phone.

'Oh, hi there,' she said.

It clearly wasn't Mum and I suffered a cold thump of fear.

'I'm fine,' said Sara. 'Honestly. I just needed a break to finish my essay.'

The caller did most of the talking and Sara rolled her eyes and made a circling motion with her forefinger. Anxiety scribbled all over me until she hung up.

'That was Dean,' she said. 'He sounds a bit off the wall.'

'Off the wall? I'd be surprised if he could find the fucking carpet,' said Phil.

Sara laughed, but I could manage no more than a hollow chuckle. Dean was still in the picture, or thought he was. Even so, I was glad the truce was holding between Sara and Phil, and that I hadn't told her about Mark. My instincts had been spot on in one area at least.

'Are you two going to be hungry? I'm afraid there isn't much here,' she said.

'Don't worry,' said Phil. 'We'll go into Pewsey and buy some stuff. Won't we, Andy?'

I readily agreed. Phil was finding it as difficult as me keeping up a front for Sara and I was scared he'd just blurt everything out. When we finished our tea, the two of us climbed back into the van.

'We can't tell her,' I said. 'We just can't, all right?'

'Chill out, we don't need to,' Phil said. 'That's what I've been wanting to tell you about. I've had a fucking great idea. Look, Richard killed Mark and tried to set us up, right?'

I nodded. 'And?'

The van's headlights swept across the garage doors.

'So now we just do it back to him. Drive Mark's body over to Foxton Hall and leave it in his garden! Let him deal with it. We turn the tables on Richard and we don't need to tell Sara or the police. Am I a genius or what?'

Lacking Phil's scalpel-sharp intellect, I wasn't immediately convinced.

'I don't know,' I said. 'Going to Richard's place with the body in the back? I don't like it. What if he recognizes the van?'

'OK, OK!' he said. 'So we drive over to take a look at Richard's place first thing tomorrow morning. Pick a spot. Then when it gets dark we go back and leave Mark for the gardener to find. You've got to admit it's good.'

Phil was exultant and the more I thought about his idea the more sense it seemed to make. I'd be able to tell Sara everything once Richard was behind bars. She'd understand, I told myself, even as the moon poked a hole through the clouds to trivialize our sense of movement along the road to Pewsey. Phil waited in the van as the comedian behind the counter in the not-so-hyper market (the sign outside read Elvis Patel at Gracelondis) scanned the barcodes of the items I'd selected with the red beam of his laser pistol. Then Phil and I retraced our tracks down the graphite road between the charcoal trees, fine-tuning our plan. The conifers loomed behind the house as a frozen tidal wave of pitch darkness against the night sky.

Sara had taken a shower and she opened the front door at my knock with wet hair, wiggling her ear to release some trapped water. She kissed me and we all went into the kitchen. The heating had begun to take the edge off the cold, but we huddled around the stove to stir-fry some noodles and talk about the past, a past that seemed so distant it might have belonged to other people. Sara recalled the time the three of us had been holed up in a Barcelona hotel room with a street full of fans outside. She mimicked Phil peeking through the net curtain and doing a head count. When Lee the drummer woke up and wandered through to our room, Phil and I had pushed him out on to the balcony in his Y-fronts and shut the door behind him without telling him about the fans in the street. He'd had to scamper along our balcony on all fours and over the parapet to his own room with two hundred teenage girls screaming at him. None of us knew what had become of Lee. He'd disappeared after discovering his name serving as an answer to a multiple-choice question on the screen of a pub trivia quiz game – a wrong answer.

'What's the difference between a drummer and a drum machine?' Phil asked.

'With a drum machine you only have to punch the information in once,' we chimed in unison.

'How many bass players does it take to change a light-bulb?' I asked.

They had forgotten the answer.

'None,' I said. 'The keyboard player can do it with his left hand.'

For a couple of hours it was almost possible to forget that Mark was lying dead in the garage, but the strain of keeping the truth from Sara began to tell and it felt to me as if we were all dancing round a bonfire on a frozen lake. Towards midnight Sara put her head on my shoulder and Phil piled more logs on the fire before climbing into the sleeping bag, zipping it up from the inside and then shutting his eyes to listen for the dead beats in his head. Hoping that he remembered about our early start in the morning, I half carried Sara up the staircase to lay her out on a double bed, spreading the cold heavy covers across her fully clothed body. I kissed her and she pulled me to her.

'You going to leave me to freeze to death?' she asked.

I thought of Mark's cold corpse outside in the garage beneath the thin sail.

'Get in,' she said.

I climbed in beside her, wearing my clothes.

'Why couldn't you just let Phil screw up on his own?' she asked. 'Let the lost lose themselves?'

Sara lay quite still, with her head on my chest and my arm around her. After a while she began to breathe more evenly and I synchronized my own breathing to help her off to sleep. I developed pins and needles in my arm but I didn't care, even as the cold-stored chill of the mattress reached my bones. I thought Sara had nodded off, but then she shifted on top of me and I felt her breast press against my ribs and her knee nuzzle my crotch. I stroked her hair and as she wriggled against me for warmth her breathing became ragged. Suddenly I felt the cold shock of her hand as a 240-volt surprise under my T-shirt. When we kissed I wanted to tell her I loved her. We moved against each other, breathing faster. Her fingers tugged my belt apart and pulled down my zip. Sara pulled her knees to her chest and slipped off her knickers to crouch on top of me, rubbing herself against me, the sheets tenting out on either side of her. It was too cold to waste any time. With blood thudding in my ears I felt Sara's fingers guide me inside her. She braced herself with her arms as I began to buck up into her, the tops of my thighs slapping at her buttocks. A boundless throb signalled my approaching orgasm and I tried to hold it back, but Sara began to swivel her hips in a circling motion and I came almost immediately.

I felt a teenage despondency but Sara seemed relaxed about it. Maybe from someone of my age she took it as a compliment. She kissed me and we held each other and later we made love again. Afterwards I looked at her in the moonlight and I wanted to squeeze inside her and for everything else to disappear.

'You don't know how much I love you,' she said.

'You what?' I asked.

'Because I don't know myself,' she added with a laugh. 'Let's go to sleep.'

My heart had turned to mush, but fortunately Sara nodded off before I had a chance to say something stupid. I lay awake for what seemed like hours, thinking about Mark's murder and the plans we'd made to avenge him. It felt to me as if Mark was right there with us in the room but I wasn't frightened. I'd been afraid of the dark as a child and when the bedroom door closed my sister and I would lie awake telling each other stories in a whisper until we became familiar with the darkness. Lying beside Sara, I was glad of the protection it offered and reached the unhappy conclusion that I'd become the bogeyman of my own childhood nightmares.

I must have fallen into a light sleep because I woke shivering in the middle of the night. The full moon shone through the window like the unwelcome torch beam of a cop the size of a cloud. I retrieved a coarse blanket and a crocheted bedcover from the floor, and it was so quiet I felt uneasy. I was used to traffic, police sirens, the thwock of a helicopter over the estate. Now all I could hear was Sara's breathing. She had a slight cold and each exhalation rasped, as though someone was twiddling the knob back and forth across an inch of short-wave radio band.

My mind had just slowed down for the soft drop back to sleep when I heard a car coming up the lane. The driver changed gear to climb the incline and then the car stopped, the handbrake cranking across the ratchet so loud and clear that it sounded as if they'd parked in the next room. I groped for my glasses, pulled on my underpants and padded down the landing, yelping in pain as I caught my hip on the corner of a dresser. The motor died and suddenly I was scared of the dark again, as scared as I'd been as a kid, or at Jeff's place just before I saw Mark's dead body for the first time.

I went into the bathroom and the tiles were cold on the soles of my feet as I looked out of the window. Some kind of Jeep was parked on the verge adjacent to the five-bar gate. The driver doused the headlights and when the faint interior light came on someone moved inside the car. A door slammed shut. Was it the police? Or Richard? Hoping it was just burglars, I ran down to the living room and shook Phil's arm. In the dying firelight his face had a strangely healthy glow, but I couldn't wake him. I heard footsteps outside and searched in vain for the poker.

Remembering the knife on the breadboard, I headed for the kitchen, but as I crossed the hallway I stubbed my toe on the cast-iron umbrella stand. Hopping on one leg, I realized we'd forgotten to lock the front door. The handle turned and the door opened. Someone stood silhouetted in the doorway. A man. He tilted his head to one side.

'Sara? It's me. Dean.'

Dean turned on the hall light and when he saw me in my underpants, the grin fell off his face faster than a guillotine and his black rat's eyes bored right into me. The bags beneath them had grown into a new set of cheeks that would soon require underwire support.

'Andy? What are you doing here?'

'I drove down with Phil,' I said.

Dean staggered forward and caught my wrist.

'Are you sleeping with her? Just tell me. I've got to know.'

His fingers dug into my flesh and despite the soft slur in his voice his anguish was genuine. I felt exposed and cold and a little sorry for him.

'Er, yes,' I said. 'I am.'

Dean released me and made a kangaroo pouch out of his lower lip. His nose was pinched and red and he rubbed at it.

'I thought so,' he sighed. 'Oh fuck, I thought so.'

I noticed the neck of a green frosted-glass brandy bottle protruding from the pocket of his blue anorak. Dean was swaying ever so slightly, like a high-rise in a gale, and his eyes pissed out a tear or two.

'I shouldn't have come down here,' he said.

'It's all right,' I said.

'I suppose I'd better go back to London. Cabin doors to automatic, know what I mean?'

'You're not going anywhere for a bit. I'll make you some coffee.'

I couldn't let him run the gauntlet with the breathalysers of at least three different constabularies. Besides, he might have killed some luckless pedestrian.

'Mark isn't here, is he?' he asked.

I fought off panic and Dean sniffed his runny nose.

'No, he's not,' I said. 'I don't know where he is.'

'He's gone missing. You haven't seen him?'

'Not since the night before last. Listen, I've got to put some clothes on,' I said.

'Is Sara upstairs?'

I told him Sara was asleep and then I went back up there to get dressed. I'd been wearing the same jeans for a week and they felt cold and greasy on my legs as I pulled them on. When Sara stirred, I told her that Dean had shown up drunk and she rubbed her eyes as it sank in. We listened to him clump around downstairs.

'The silly twit,' she said. 'Don't worry, Andy. It's been over for ages. Put him to sleep in one of the spare rooms, would you? I can't face talking to him.'

Hearing music downstairs, I went to lend Phil some support and found him with Dean in the living room. Phil was finding our unexpected visitor heavy going and any sympathy I'd felt for Dean quickly evaporated. As he banged on about a commercial he was planning to make in Mexico, I fantasized about the intractable bacillus he would contract from a roadside tortilla, the minimal hygiene standards of the corrugated-iron shed that would serve as his hospital and the treatment he'd receive at the hands of an unreconstructed Marxist-Leninist intern.

'I wish I knew where Mark's got to. Did he say anything to you?' Dean asked Phil.

'He was gone by the time I got up,' Phil said.

Dean's eyebrows jerked up and when his glasses slid down his nose he pushed them back up it.

'But I thought you said he left around lunch time.'

Phil's mouth opened to no effect. It was just another hole in his head.

'Phil doesn't get up much before three,' I said.

'Do you know where he went?' Dean asked. 'He owes me money, you see. And I'm a bit strapped at the minute.'

'I've no idea,' I said. 'I left early to go to work.'

I sensed the cross-hairs aligning on the garage and was beginning to regret stashing the corpse in there. What if we couldn't get Mark out? The two of them punished the brandy and I watched while it punished them straight back, blow for blow. Dean's eyes closed but Phil barely noticed, having long been reduced to a grunt himself. I reminded him that we had to set off early in the morning and went back upstairs and climbed into bed with Sara. If the opportunity arose, I wanted to move Mark's body from the garage and hide it in the woods before we left. Accordingly I banged my head against the pillow six times. It made a welcome change from a brick wall.

I woke beside Sara and the slatted wooden blind admitted a rack of light that crossed the carpet and climbed on to the bed to curve over her naked back. It was already nine o'clock and even though I'd overslept I was filled with rare happiness. The window sparkled with condensation, so I got out of bed, wrote our initials on the pane and wiped them away. And then I saw the garage through the cleared glass and the thought of its contents brought me up sharp. Dean had made it to a bedroom down the landing. His gym-body had become a temple, a temple of doom, and I watched him toss and turn as he fought off imaginary assailants in his sleep. His bedroom overlooked the garage, so we couldn't risk moving Mark's body. A needling bladder or a wakeful pang of remorse from Dean, one little 'oh no!', and Phil and I could easily end up on a murder charge. I saw myself in the dock as the judge pronounced sentence, gazing up at the public gallery, where a tearful Sara would be consoled by Dean Haas.

I tiptoed down the stairs so as not to wake Dean, struggling to suppress my renascent smoker's cough. In the living room Phil's white arm trailed from the orange sleeping bag and each time he snored his fingers prodded a packet of Marlboro on the carpet, as if his hand was intent on a little sleep-smoking. I went into the kitchen, filled the electric kettle and searched for a mug and a tea-bag. The kettle rumbled to a click as Phil came into the kitchen, still reeling from the daily reminder of who he was, fingers grubbing at his frightful hair as he recomposed his personality.

'How's it going?' I asked.

'I think it's gone.'

'Keep your voice down,' I said. 'It's already bloody nine o'clock. What do we do about Mark?'

'Leave him in the garage, I suppose. Pick out somewhere to dump him at Richard's place and hope we can move him tonight.'

Phil scratched his neck.

'Look, I've been thinking,' he said. 'Maybe Sara was in on it with Richard.'

'Don't be daft!' I said.

We had enough to worry about without indulging in paranoid fantasy.

'What if she tells Dean about the stamps and everything?' he asked.

'She won't,' I said.

Struggling to secure the loose cargo on the deck of my own mind, I handed Phil a mug of tea (the dirtier one, in accordance with his slapdash approach to matters of hygiene), and as soon as he'd gulped it down we free-wheeled the van back on to the lane and drove off towards Pewsey. With any luck we'd be back with the newspapers before the others knew we were gone.

17

Sunlight slashed through the branches of the trees at the side of the road and at the top of a rise a quilt of woods and fields spread out before us. I wasn't used to such distances or to so much chlorophyll. Most of my life had been in black and white or at best a suburban sepia, more Evostik with Tracy than Cider with Rosie, but this didn't stop me imagining a life in the country with Sara. A life involving a duck pond and possibly some organic goats. Health. Early nights. Children. Then I thought of Mark and the test-tube dream smashed on the laboratory bench. Phil picked up his Omnichord and fiddled with the dictaphone attachment.

'For fuck's sake, Phil, put it away. I can't take it this early. Or ever.'

I'd hit a nerve. He put down the Omnichord and sat bolt upright, round-eyed as some fresh consternation blew down the canyons of his mind.

'D'you think I'm too old for it?' he asked. 'Have I lost it? Tell me the truth.'

We were an inch away from prison and Phil was still worried about his career prospects, but he was as defenceless as a snail dispossessed of its shell and I had to tread carefully. I didn't want him falling apart on me.

'Course not,' I said.

'I've slipped too far behind, haven't I?'

'Behind what? It's not a race. There's no bloke with a chequered flag.'

Phil didn't seem to hear a word I said. He had a big head, but the minute he stopped pumping it up it shrank to the size of a pea.

'Do you think I'm a loser?' he asked.

'All those people trying to buy themselves the best pair of blinkers, they're the losers if anyone is. Running round the track till their batteries give out.'

I'd almost convinced myself and he sat there thinking about it.

'There's life after death, Andy.'

'You know that for sure?'

'Yeah. I looked at Mark's face going blue and I realized he'd gone somewhere else. That he'd moved on. His energy, you know.'

'He hasn't got much energy right now, unless St Peter pushes diet pills on the door.'

'I'm serious. For most of the time we're not alive, are we? We're somewhere else. In time, sort of thing. So this isn't our normal state. It's fucking brilliant!'

Phil treated me to a fatuous smile before retreating into the silence of a smug voyant as we approached the outskirts and then the very petticoat of Pewsey. I was afraid to ask a local for directions to Foxton Hall in case they might remember us later. Like in the run-up to Richard's murder trial. I could all too easily imagine some bibulous hayseed being coached by one of Richard's forty-strong defence team into putting us away for fifteen years. The newsagent's looked a likely source for an Ordnance Survey map, so I parked the van, feeling like a town rat in my paint-splashed jeans. Phil struck an equally crusty chord as we walked over paving stones so rounded and rustic that they might have been laid by Hobbits. A red-faced man in a tweed jacket observed us from a bus shelter.

'He's looking at us,' Phil whispered.

We struggled to act natural as we entered the newsagent's but it was like stepping back half a century. The man buying pipe tobacco from the granny behind the counter looked as assured as David Niven and I envied him his apparent peace of mind. Jars of lemon sherbets and barley sugar lined one wall, the kind of sweets you bought by net weight, not weight of advertising. On a shelf above some puzzle magazines, I found a map that covered Pewsey and the surrounding area. While I waited in line behind the rural pipe-head, Phil flicked through the local paper and I saw from the front page that a nearby town was suffering something of a crime wave. At the weekend two teenagers had set fire to a post box and had been fined a hundred pounds by the magistrate. My own rag usually offered up some poor pensioner stabbed for 47p and left for dead, so I felt a long way from home. Arcane cigarette brands like Sweet Afton were displayed alongside the machine brands, the big corporate killers: Philip Morris, Peter Stuyvesant, Alfred Dunhill. The Bundys behind the bike sheds.

The pipe-smoker and the granny took for ever to complete their transaction, reinforcing each other's conviction that it was indeed a lovely day. If they kept it up for much longer, the day was going to get ideas and call itself a week, and every extra second I spent in the shop cranked my fears up another notch. What if Richard Bowring came into the shop? On the radio a DJ warned of some roadworks outside Marlborough and informed us that twenty-five miles of ice cube had just dropped off Antarctica. Then he congratulated a couple on the birth of their baby and played their request, the soundtrack to their courtship. I was already so fraught that when I heard the DJ say the word 'Overload' in his West Country accent, I thought I was hallucinating.

He played 'Waterbed', our singular hit.

As the first few bars sounded I felt my head explode. The chord progression ADADAE seemed Dymo-taped into my very DNA. Phil gaped at me as we listened to his past self sing the words I'd first written on the back of a Kentucky Fried Chicken carton with the aftertaste of the Colonel's secret recipe spoiling my mouth as the Transit van sped down a dual carriageway in somewhere like Lincolnshire. It all came back to me: the grease spots on the white cardboard above my field of rollerpoint scrawl; my body aching all over; the dream of a hot bath and sleep.

It was the first time I'd heard the song in eight months. Phil was staring open-mouthed at the radio.

'Remember this one? Nice tune,' the pipe-smoker said to the granny.

'Mmm. Sounds a bit like that new Jamiroquai thingy,' the granny replied.

I thought I was losing my mind. When the pipe-smoker left the shop the granny tried to keep her smile going, but she sensed something awry and her eyes flicked from me to Phil and back again. She was in her mid-sixties, but as I stepped up to the counter I noticed that she was wearing Tommy Hilfiger track-suit bottoms and fluorescent trainers beneath her nylon pinny. Phil was shaking and I paid for the map and a packet of Superkings and bundled him back on to the street as the song went into the middle eight.

'Fuck, Andy. That was too much,' he said. 'That was a message from Mark!'

'It was just a coincidence.'

'Come off it. When did you last hear it on the radio?' he asked.

I pretended to scour my mind for the memory, even though it was still razor sharp: the pub in Gospel Oak, the barman's flicker of recognition and my acute sense of embarrassment.

'Um, a couple of months ago,' I said. 'It doesn't mean anything.'

'Yeah, it does! You'll see! It means Mark's looking out for us.'

'That's bollocks. Look out for yourself,' I said.

We walked back to the van, trying to blend in, smiling at our fellow pedestrians. Neighbourliness (or suspicion) went a little further in the country, but as soon as we were safely encased in the rotting body of the van, I spread the map over the steering wheel and found that Richard owned a sizeable chunk of England's green and solid land. Foxton Hall was on the edge of a village on the far side of Pewsey, or rather the village was on the edge of Foxton Hall. We set off and got stuck for a while behind a slow-moving pick-up with an old sticker in the back window promoting the countryside march. It read 'Listen to us', but the driver drove alone and in silence. Overtaking it, I narrowly avoided road-killing a white-haired dog-walker, and I saw her shaking a stick at me in the mirror before she dropped into the ditch.

'Stupid old bat,' said Phil. 'It's not your fault there aren't any bloody pavements.'

After a couple of miles we found ourselves circling a long stone wall that surrounded some woods.

'This is Richard's place,' I said.

'What, the forest and everything?'

*

The wall curved back from the main road towards some iron gates that stood open. On a small gate house a peeling sign said PRIVATE, the red letters faded to the shade of anti-rust paint. Below it in black: NO PUBLIC RIGHT OF WAY. I pulled on to a fan of loose gravel just as a van bearing the Interflora symbol emerged from the gates. I braked hard, my bald tyres tearing at the stones as the florist headed off in the direction of Pewsey. I'd just put the van back into gear when a Land Rover barrelled out of the gates and I caught a glimpse of Richard Bowring's tanned profile beneath a brown hat.

Petrified, I squashed myself down into the footwell, my adrenal gland tenderizing my neck and shoulders. Phil swore and I told him to shut up. My ears were pricked, waiting for the Land Rover to scrunch to a stop, for the door to slam and for the sound of Richard's footsteps to get louder until his hand yanked open the door of my van. Mercifully, Richard pulled out on to the road and accelerated, and I raised my head millimetre by millimetre to peer through a hoop of steering wheel as the back of the Land Rover shrank away to nothing. Overjoyed to see Richard disappear, Phil raised his hand and (though it now shames me to admit it) I mirrored his ludicrous high-five.

'What do you reckon?' I asked. 'Do we go in?'

'Course! It couldn't be better. Maybe our luck's changing.'

It was the first genuine smile I'd seen on Phil's face for a while and I followed the drive into the trees, braking on account of a gentle speed bump set into the tarmac. The drive went deep into the woods, and even though I'd seen it on the map I was surprised at the size of the place. After a hundred and fifty yards we turned sharply to the left and began to descend a shallow slope. I was expecting to see the house, but the woods became even denser. I'd no idea what make of trees they were and I still don't, but some of them were beginning to sprout pale-green leaves. Older-looking trees with thicker trunks stood among them, bent out of shape and fuzzed with moss and lichen. At the side of the drive two enormous mushrooms were growing out of a rotten log. The pot-holed roadway narrowed and the branches of the trees scraped at the side of the van, joining overhead to cut out much of the light. I began to feel uneasy.

'I've seen enough,' I said. 'We can come back tonight and leave the body in these woods.'

'Come on,' Phil said. 'Keep going for a bit. Maybe there's somewhere better up ahead.'

I drove on, clinging to the hope that Phil was right about our change of luck.

'Hang on,' he said. 'Who's that?'

An old man was walking down the drive some forty feet in front of us and when he saw the van he waved. I wanted to throw the van into reverse and get out of there, but Phil insisted that we try to bluff it out.

'So we took a wrong turn. What's he going to do? Shoot us?'

I thought Phil was getting cocky, but I didn't fancy having to reverse back up the winding drive and so I stayed put. The man's footsteps squelched in the mud as he approached the passenger window. His face was so weathered that it looked as if he'd taken to leaving it outside overnight.

'Sorry, I think we could be lost,' Phil said.

The man looked kindly upon us.

'You for Foxton Hall? You'll be wanting the main house. Just keep on up the drive.'

'Thanks,' said Phil.

The man touched the brim of his cap with a hand as chapped as an old bar of soap and I drove on. I didn't understand quite how it had happened, but it seemed we were in the clear.

'See? I told you,' said Phil. 'Piece of piss.'

To the left a stretch of parkland swept down to a stream and then we saw the house itself, a stark white bulk high up on the rise. The drive switchbacked to the left and we came out of the trees on to an apron of raked yellow gravel. The house had three storeys and then another smaller one with dormer windows above a sort of parapet. Up close you could see that the building was in need of repair. Some time soon a contractor was going to make a killing and it was obvious that the place must have cost a bomb to maintain. There was a red-brick stable block at the back of the house and Richard Bowring's 'performance' sports car was parked by the stables, a sharp flat reminder as to why we were there. A marquee covered half the lawn on the far side of the house and several commercial vans were parked near it. People were carrying chairs into the tent.

'The old bloke must've thought we were workmen,' said Phil. 'You fitted right in, Andy! We could bring the body here and leave it in the marquee.'

It was a lucky break and I felt the tension lift from my shoulders. For the first time since Norwood, I really began to think we might be going to get away with it. Phil wanted to take a look around and I agreed, crawling across the gravel in first gear to park about twenty feet beyond the last of the other vans. There was a smell of sawn wood on the breeze.

18

When we got out of the van a stable lad was coming in our direction, carrying a rubber bucket and a pink sponge, so we less stable men moved away towards some rhododendron bushes that bordered the lawn. Inside the marquee the caterers were setting up tables and gold plastic chairs with red cushions, gang-mastered by a matron wearing a headscarf that bore an equestrian motif. A young girl with a brown ponytail walked past us, carrying a plastic crate full of glasses. Phil smiled at her.

'All right?' he said.

To his evident satisfaction and my astonishment, she smiled back at him. A microphone stood on a dais at the far end of the marquee, presumably for Richard's presentation the next day, and it reminded me of the time we'd played in a marquee at an Oxford University May Ball, one of our worst gigs. Good money, but the audience wasn't interested in the band and after two songs they tried to jeer us off, hungry for the disco and the rub of hired dinner suit against taffeta. Although you could hardly blame them given the sound we made, the sight of the gilded piglets at play was still enough to make you want to join Class War.

I scanned the marquee for something makeshift or last-minute that might reveal the disorder in Richard's mind, but everything seemed so well organized that it was hard to reconcile the scene with Mark's murder, a crime to make the sky rain blood. The matron flashed her nostrils at us, and when it began to look as if she might actually whinny we left the marquee. I followed Phil along the side of the house, past a stone statue of an ancient female naturist, and through a window we saw a portly Asian man sitting reading a paper. He was dressed in a tweed suit and the only things missing were the monocle and the pink gin. He waved at us and we waved back. It was all going swimmingly.

'What did I tell you? Our luck's changed,' Phil said.

We drove away from there exultant and Phil started singing Bryan Adams's '18 Till I Die', the way he'd done when things were going well in the band. As we headed down the drive, I took a corner a little too fast and when the drive switchbacked to the right, the van skidded.

'Watch it!' cried Phil.

I fought to keep it under control, turning the wheel into the skid.

The Land Rover was coming up the drive in the opposite direction. I had the van more or less back on track, but I didn't see the Land Rover until we were on top of it. The drive was too narrow for two vehicles to pass, so I swerved to the left, where the trees were smaller and newer. I hit the brakes and the rear end of the van swung away to the left. Low branches battered the windscreen. Twisting the wheel to no effect, I saw the big tree looming fast, the trunk widening and the crevices visible in the bark the moment before impact.

The next thing I knew, I was smelling earth and rotting wood, lying face down, literally digging the nature scene with my chin.

My teeth were loose and I could taste blood in my mouth. Something was very wrong with my left shoulder and it strobed with pain when I tried to move it – the

bright, heart-stopping agony of a childhood bicycle accident – as if my arm had been twisted and torn out of the
shoulder socket and the socket was now busy cutting a set
of teeth. Inwards. I lay there whimpering, praying for the
pain to go away, but my shoulder continued to beat like a
second heart.

I'd lost my glasses, so I couldn't see too well, but I
thought I could make out Richard Bowring kneeling over
Phil and shaking him, a few yards from the tree that we'd
crashed against. I put my right hand to my forehead and
my fingers came away wet with blood. Scratches, I
thought. Cuts. From the windscreen? I assessed my skull
for damage with the nervous fingers of a bomb-disposal
expert, wincing as I found the supersensitive point of
impact on top of my head. Richard came over to me, lower-
ing his face within range of my short sight.

'What the hell are you doing here?' he asked.

There was a dark-brown mole in the centre of his chin,
and the mole had a dimple in it from which a solitary hair
protruded, curled and black, like the stalk of a decom-
posed apple. There was a patch of skin at the side of his
mouth that he'd missed with the razor and grey hairs bris-
tled in the satsuma pores. I pointed to Phil and tried to say
his name. It took me for ever to shape the word.

'Is this something to do with Mark?' Richard barked.

He knew full well it was to do with Mark. Was he acting
it up for someone else's benefit? Perhaps there'd been a
passenger in the Land Rover.

'Ambulance,' I said. 'Get an ambulance.'

Phil cried out and Richard went over to him. I couldn't
move without making my shoulder worse, so I tried to
keep as still as possible. Then a dog put its face in mine,
growling at me from deep inside itself, and I was seized by

Stone Age terror. I looked up into dark eyes that wanted to swallow me whole. Black and tan pelt and pointed ears, framed by the branches of the overhanging trees. Good brand recognition: Dobermann. The teeth might have been arrayed and sharpened with my exact neck measurement in mind. Steam came off the dog's long, pink tongue and blew across a tiny range of rubbery black gum nodules that were slick with drool. Beyond the tongue I could see the beginning of the ribbed hose of the throat. Just as I felt the food chain tighten round my neck and start to pull in the other direction, Richard wrenched the dog away to replace its face with his own. He was breathing too hard and hanks of grey hair flapped over his ears. He looked very tired.

'Where's Mark? What happened?'

I didn't know whether to challenge him or to play dumb. Or dumber. I remembered throwing Mark's shoe into the back of the van. It was still there. My right hand brushed against my glasses in the leaves and I managed to put them on.

'I dunno what you're talking about,' I mumbled.

'What have you done with Mark? My wife told me you're a friend of his. Where is he?'

He shook me and the sudden pain pushed me down into a pool of squid ink and left me there.

I came round to see two Richards with four lapels, beneath a double dose of sky fish-netted by a thousand broken branches. Both rows of teeth jiggled on the left side of my face and the inside of my mouth was outsize and full of blood. I decided I'd better swallow it to save the protein, because I had the feeling I was going to need all the strength I could get. I was a child again, rattling the teeth in the bleached skull of a sheep on holiday in Suffolk. I was a fool.

'Where's Mark?' Richard asked me.

My only chance was to overpower him, but with what I took to be concussion and one arm out of commission the odds looked even slimmer than my share portfolio. And then I looked past Richard to see Phil's legs sticking out of the passenger door of the Land Rover. It was green with a cream roof – I'd had a toy one just like it as a kid. Phil was groping for something in the back and I had a stab at a death rattle to distract Richard, spluttering the blood from my gums, but it wasn't enough. The Dobermann barked and ran flat out at Phil.

'Get him, Rolf!' Richard shouted.

Phil twisted out of the cab, his face flecked with blood. With fluke timing, he kicked out and sank a boot into the dog's chest a split second before the canine's canines buried themselves in his throat. The dog shot straight up in the air and landed on its feet to stand quite still for a moment in a state of utter surprise. Richard was moving towards Phil, but suddenly he stopped as if he'd come to the edge of a cliff. Phil held a shotgun levelled at his chest. There was a gust of wind in the trees and sunlight filled the clearing. Richard's russet jacket seemed to burst into flames.

No one moved.

Phil looked crazed enough to shoot and I hoped that the shotgun had a stiff trigger. His face had been cut badly and a flap of skin hung off his brow; blood had run out of it to soak into his T-shirt.

'Be sensible. Put the gun down,' Richard said, squeezing the words out through gritted teeth.

'You toffee-nosed shite!' Phil yelled. 'I should fucking shoot you now!'

'Steady,' I said.

I was shocked by the force of Phil's hatred and remembered the time they'd met in the dining room in Regent's Park.

'Get that bloody dog away or I'll kill it!' Phil shouted.

Richard called Rolf back and made him sit.

'You're making this worse for yourself,' said Richard.

Phil raised the shotgun to his shoulder and took a step towards Richard. The barrels were pointing straight at Richard's head, a silver infinity symbol floating in midair.

'For fuck's sake, Phil! Don't!' I shouted.

Phil lowered the gun and limped back to lean against the Land Rover. He was in a bad way.

'Where's Mark? What have you done with him?' Richard asked.

The question hung in the crisp air of the clearing. I didn't get it. Was Richard asking what we'd done with the body? Or was he just acting? Phil winced at some sudden pain and the barrels of the gun drifted momentarily away from Richard. Then Phil staggered and I saw Richard tense as he prepared to make another move.

'Watch him, Phil,' I said.

'I'm all right. It's just my leg. Can you get up?' he asked me.

The dog bolted.

'Phil! Look!' I yelled.

The Dobermann leapt at Phil, getting its teeth into his forearm. Phil screamed as he clubbed the shotgun down, cracking the barrels hard on to the dog, until Rolf shrieked and dragged himself off into the trees, yelping like a car alarm. Richard didn't move and Phil put the gun back on him, panting and rubbing his arm.

'The RSPCA's not going to like that one bit,' I said.

'The RSPCA's the least of our worries,' Phil replied.

*

I winched myself to my feet and everything went wavery, but I managed to wedge my hand between the buttons of my coat to take the weight off my shoulder. I stumbled towards Phil and felt as though I was swimming across a choppy Channel, goggled and smeared with grease. Phil beckoned Richard over to the Land Rover and when Richard opened his mouth to speak, Phil slammed the butt of the shotgun into his back. Richard went down, gasping for breath, and held on to the tailgate. I was horrified, but I kept my mouth shut as the ramifications of our situation started to unfold inside me, spikier than a Swiss Army knife.

'Take this, will you?' Phil asked me.

He handed me the shotgun and I pointed it at Richard while Phil rummaged in the Land Rover's first aid box for a strip of plaster to patch his eyebrow. When he'd finished, he checked his handiwork in the side-mirror and made a little crinkle-cut smile. I was stunned. How could Phil be smiling? With his colossal vanity? He hobbled over to my van and my shoulder throbbed alarmingly as I stood there holding the gun on Richard. If he'd jumped me, there was no way I could have pulled the trigger or even hit him with it, but luckily for me, Richard remained on his hands and knees panting for air, busy enacting *Lassie Come Home* ('whole thing') in a game of charades. Phil retrieved his portable keyboard from the wreckage of the van and returned.

'We've got to get him to confess,' Phil whispered to me.

I was puzzled. Did Phil plan to inflict his songs on Richard to force a confession? As an interrogation technique it would make Torquemada look like David Frost. Phil untaped his dictaphone from the keyboard, rewound the tiny cassette, and then took me aside.

– 178 –

'We'll get him away from here. Force him to admit it on tape,' he said.

'I don't see –'

'Well, we can't just leave him here, can we?'

Phil was right about that and I knew enough to know I wasn't thinking straight. He tied Richard's hands behind his back with some orange plastic string he'd found in the back of the Land Rover and I tried to help as best I could, but with only one arm and skewed vision I probably only hindered him.

'Where's Rolf?' Richard moaned.

Phil told him to shut up. The dog lay whimpering at the base of a tree, dying for all I knew. Phil found some newsprint in the footwell, stuffed it into Richard's mouth and put a green fertilizer bag twice the size of a pillowcase over his head, and then we lifted him into the back of the Land Rover. Darkness crowded in at the periphery, as if I was looking at the world down a pair of shotgun barrels, and Phil asked me if I could handle the Land Rover with my arm in a sling.

'I keep fading in and out,' I said. 'I'd probably crash on a main road. Why don't we just push into the woods a bit? Get away from the drive?'

Phil took a close look at me and agreed. We climbed into the cab and Phil dabbed at his still-bleeding face with an old dishcloth as I attempted to find first gear with my right arm. I grappled with the stick and when it finally clanked into place we shot forwards through the trees to the sound of branches scraping on metal. Worried that I'd get stuck and be unable to turn round, I made painfully slow progress. Richard wriggled on the floor behind us and I started out of my seat before I remembered that, unlike Mark, this Bowring was still alive. Phil yelled a warning as

I hit a ditch and almost tipped us over, but eventually we came into another small clearing at the edge of a field and I pulled to a stop. When I got out of the cab I couldn't see my van for the trees, so I assumed we couldn't be seen from the drive.

19

My left arm had gone numb and I was getting light-headed, so Phil helped me fashion a sling from the dish-cloth, which depicted Charles and Diana on the day of their engagement. I tried not to take this much-machine-washed veronica as a curse on my relationship with Sara. How could I ever explain all this to her? I tried to push these thoughts aside as Phil set up his dictaphone on the Land Rover's bonnet and tested it, his breathy one-two, one-two recalling countless enervating sound-checks in sheds and halls up and down the country. The microphone had a range of about five feet. He played it back and reset the machine with the same jerky uncertainty that I'd first noticed in the pub in Clerkenwell.

'It's a shame we can't show him Mark's body before we start,' Phil said. 'Soften him up.'

'Soften him up? Mark was his son,' I said. 'It'd liquefy him.'

Phil dragged Richard half-way out of the Land Rover with the fertilizer bag still over his head, untied his legs and bundled him upright as a cut-price pantomime beanstalk. Richard made a croaking sound as Phil pushed him to the ground and tied his hands to the front bumper, setting up for the strangest recording session I'd ever been involved in. I had a bad sense of foreboding and I'm not just being wise after the event. Phil started the tiny tape spooling behind Richard's back and then he pulled the bag off his head with a flourish.

Richard's face had turned a nasty reddish-brown colour and I remembered Ildikó telling me about his heart condition. When I mentioned this to Phil, he looked worried too – the last thing we needed was another dead body on our hands, and Richard's eyes bulged frog-like as Phil pulled the pulped pages from his mouth. Spitting out the last of the paper, Richard exploded with indignation.

'Shut the fuck up!' Phil shouted.

He raised an arm and Richard cowered.

'All right,' said Phil. 'First you can tell us why didn't you go to the police when you heard about Mark.'

Richard was surprised at the question and, to my eyes, he looked a little guilty.

'I wanted to call them but my wife persuaded me not to.'

'It was because you'd ripped off Mark's trust fund, wasn't it?'

'That's preposterous!' Richard scoffed. 'Listen, is Mark here? Is he involved in this? I have a right to know.'

Richard had all the integrity of a resprayed BMW, but his arrogance gave me a bad feeling. Even kneeling in the mud, Richard was still a big-shot landowner, whereas we were a pair of lumpen proles who'd brought his son's corpse down from London. I couldn't see Richard admitting to a thing. And when it came to murder, possession of the body was surely nine-tenths of the law.

'Why don't you tell us why you killed him?' Phil asked.

Richard looked as if someone had thrown a glass of water in his face and his breathing became fast and shallow. Once again I was mindful of his heart condition.

'You're saying Mark's . . . dead?'

Richard's words clogged in his throat. That's when I

had my first real inkling that he hadn't done it.

'I-I don't understand,' Richard stuttered.

That stuttered 'I' crashed like a sawn tree to thump down on the muddy ground in front of me, but Phil didn't see it and he redoubled his attack.

'Course you bloody understand!' he shouted. 'You went round to the flat and you smashed Mark's head in!'

Richard didn't get it. He looked like a frail, persecuted old man.

'What happened at Kilburn?' I asked Richard.

'Kilburn? I've never even been to Kilburn,' he said.

'Come off it!' Phil snapped.

Richard shook his head and I couldn't understand why he'd bother to lie about that.

'I saw you there myself,' I said. 'After you went to the train station. You were in your car.'

'But I didn't have my car that day,' Richard said. 'I used taxis.'

My windpipe sealed up, flat as a tapeworm, and I gulped to prise it apart.

'Then who had it?' I asked. 'Who was driving it?'

Something seemed to burst behind Richard's face.

'My wife. Her car was in the garage,' he said, looking away.

I remembered Emma telling me she was taking her car in to be fixed. Richard hadn't done it. I felt faint.

'You're fucking lying!' Phil yelled at him.

Phil hit him right on the ear, but Richard didn't seem to feel a thing. I grabbed Phil and pulled him back.

'Leave him alone!' I shouted. 'He's telling the truth! Listen to me! How do we know it wasn't Emma? With Mark dead and Richard's dodgy ticker, she's looking at eight million quid.'

Phil pulled free of me and Richard looked as if he was in shock.

'No way,' Phil said. 'She'd have told me, all right?'

I took a step back. It didn't make sense.

'What do you mean, she'd have told you?' I asked. 'You don't even bloody know her!'

Phil took a deep breath and let it out.

'The girl in LA I told you about? Emma. We're getting back together. Like it was before but better. I love her, Andy.'

My mind was stuck in the mud, the rear wheels churning up the first wave of a massive panic attack. Crushed and pulled apart by the contradictory demands of claustrophobia and agoraphobia, I tried to open a window in my lungs for some fresh air, but they were all stuck. It was like trying to breathe through a pillow.

'Look, it's all right. It doesn't change anything,' Phil said. 'Emma doesn't even know Mark's dead.'

'You've seen her?' I asked, horror-struck.

'I talked to her on the phone when you were round there yesterday. I was going to tell you.'

'You slimy fucking little maggot!'

'I had to call her,' Phil said. 'She knew it was me on the phone the other day and with Mark dead I didn't want her telling Richard she was leaving him. Not yet anyway.'

Phil had been lying the whole time, to me and to himself. I hated him and the hatred helped me to beat back the panic attack. It was all too clear to me what had happened.

'Can't you see Emma did it?' I snarled. 'She killed Mark and set you up for it, you fucking moron!'

Phil staggered back from an invisible blow.

'That's a lie!' Richard wailed.

'Yeah, that's a load of crap!' Phil cried. 'She thought I

was making the calls to wind her up! To get her to ask for the divorce. She'd no idea Mark was round at Jeff's!'

'Come on,' I said to Phil. 'You know she did it.'

Phil's mouth opened and closed. He was losing it, wrestling with suspicions that he'd been unable to acknowledge in himself. Richard's face was mottled and he was shaking. Neither of them wanted to believe me, but for once I knew I was right.

'She couldn't have. She didn't know the address in Kilburn,' Richard said, an octave too high. 'She'd gone out by the time the girl called. I told the police and they said they went there but the flat was empty.'

That knocked me back.

'See?' said Phil. 'Emma had nothing to do with it! He bloody did the murder himself, just like we thought!'

'No! Mark's alive!' cried Richard.

'You want to see the body?' Phil sneered. 'It's in a garage five miles up the road.'

At that moment Richard knew for certain that his son was dead. He groaned and hid his face in his shoulder, caught in a sandstorm of feeling, inadvertently revealing a bald spot on his crown that he usually combed over. I was confused. I couldn't figure out how Emma had discovered Jeff's address.

'You ever take Emma over to Kilburn?' I asked Phil.

His eyes burrowed deeper beneath the protective shelf of his bandaged brow.

'I told you I stayed there when I got back from LA. She spent a few nights with me. So what?'

'Did you ever take her round to Hammersmith?'

'Course not. You've seen what a tip it is.'

'So she thought you lived at Jeff's. And she went round to stop you making the calls and found Mark. They fought over something and she killed him. She set you up, Phil. With Mark dead, she gets the money.'

Phil couldn't hold my gaze. He thumped the Land Rover's bonnet with his fist.

'That's crap. Emma's not bothered about money,' he said.

'Yeah, sure. Why d'you think she married Richard? His warm, loving nature? It's eight million quid, you twerp.'

Richard moaned, grey and deflated. When I went over to check on him, he looked up at me with poisoned eyes.

'Untie me,' he croaked. 'Please. My hands hurt.'

Richard's fingers were developing the same bluish tinge as his son's, so I loosened his wrists a little. Life was going out of him like grain pouring out of a sack, and it was the first time I'd ever felt the slightest bit of sympathy for a property developer. Then I heard a car coming, closer than I'd have liked. Crows flew off across the field and a flash of blue bodywork glinted through the trees forty yards away. I glimpsed a black canvas roof as the car headed up the drive towards the main house.

'That's Emma,' said Phil.

I thought he was going to run after her and I got ready to trip him, but he didn't budge. We heard the car stop by the van and we waited until Emma drove on.

'How long do you think she'd stay with you without money?' I asked Phil. 'She'll sell you out the first chance she gets.'

'You don't know a thing. Emma's going to leave him. She told me so yesterday.'

'Only so you'd get rid of the body for her,' I said.

'She'd never hurt Mark,' Richard mumbled. 'She'd never hurt him.'

The repetition made it sound like the lie it was, a sentimental lie. Phil was looking shaky. I realized that Emma had fucked me only to try and find out how much I knew, so I turned on Phil, anxious to put that particular stick in his spokes.

'Emma didn't care if you ditched the body or you got caught,' I told him. 'Whichever way, she's in the clear and she gets the money. Christ, you really think she cares about you? She even fucked me yesterday, just to try and find out what we'd done with Mark!'

Phil stepped towards me and hit me on the side of the head. I was more surprised than anything, because he was such a coward, but maybe his last heartstring had broken inside him. I was expecting him to swing at me again, so I was wrong-footed when he grabbed a handful of my hair and buried his fingers follicle-deep. I broke free and belted him right on the ribs, directly over his heart.

I knocked him back against the Land Rover, held him there, squeezing his throat with my right hand, and kicked at him. Phil's own left arm was as useless as mine, on account of the dog-bite. Richard was shouting something but it sounded far away, in the next village. Phil struggled to free himself and when he started body-punching me, I managed to keep my damaged shoulder out of range until his blows weakened. Phil's face began to get some colour for once as he scrabbled to pull my left arm from the sling. When that didn't work, he reached inside the cab for the shotgun. I took a step back and kicked the side of his knee as hard as I could. He screamed.

'Fuck you, Andy! That's my bad leg!' he howled, hopping on his other one.

I retrieved the shotgun from the Land Rover and went over to Richard. Kneeling on the ground, he looked as if he was being slowly swallowed by the earth and didn't mind at all. I untied him and he rubbed at his freed wrists, rose unsteadily to his feet and took a few big-eyed steps like an air-crash survivor picking his way through the wreckage. He was quite unrecognizable from the strutting bully of Regent's Park.

'I knew something dreadful had happened when she came home,' he said, not so much to me as to some inner interlocutor. 'There was a mark on her neck. She tried to cover it up, but I saw.'

I told Richard to tie Phil's hands behind his back with the baler twine and then tie his ankles together.

'Hang on a minute! What are you doing?' Phil shrieked at me. 'You're mad! Richard killed Mark, remember?'

'That's not true!' Richard roared, shoving Phil face down on the ground.

I pulled the old man back.

'What the fuck are you doing, Andy?' Phil howled. 'He's trying to con you!'

'She'd never hurt Mark,' said Richard. 'She loves him as much as I do.'

'For fuck's sake, Andy, let me go!' Phil yelled. 'Can't you see it's all just an act?'

'That's rich coming from you! You fucking lied to me all the way along!'

Richard wrapped the twine round Phil's wrists and Phil kept yelling, so I shoved some newsprint in his mouth. When Richard had finished, I found more twine and tied him up the same way. It wasn't easy with only one hand and I didn't do a very good job, but I figured he was too disoriented to pose much of a threat. I had to break off every so often to get my breath back.

'I need to see my son,' Richard said.

'Everything'll be all right,' I lied. 'I'm going to get help.'

My only chance was to trick Emma into a confession. I rewound the dictaphone and as I climbed into the Land Rover I heard Phil yelping through the gag, sounding like a clubbed seal pup. I hoped Richard had tied him up properly, but even if he hadn't I didn't think Phil would get far on his bad leg. Taking great care, I drove back to the drive through the wood. The front end of my van was stubbed right into the fat tree and when I saw it up close, I realized how lucky Phil and I were to be alive, because when it came to the van, you were your own crumple zone, your own air-bag. I thought about retrieving Mark's shoe from the van but I didn't have the energy so I pushed on up to the house in first gear, not bothering to shift, making the engine screech. Emma's convertible was parked beside Richard's sports car at the top of the drive.

20

I stepped into the house through a side door by the kitchen. The hallway smelt of dogs and the mouldered rubber of wellington boots. Coats hung along a wall from which the floral paper had peeled to flop over faded prints of hunting scenes in thin frames. Tennis racquets, umbrellas and shooting sticks gathered dust in a stand. I opened a door into a kitchen and told an anaemic put-upon woman that I'd crashed on the drive and that I needed to speak to Emma Bowring. I was covered in mud and my face might as well have been minced by the food processor that gleamed on the sideboard, so the woman took some convincing that I didn't need an ambulance before she dialled Emma on an internal line.

She stared at me and I stared at a ray of sunlight that caught a million motes on its way to illuminate the exposed beams of the country-style kitchen. The woman asked me to leave my mud-caked trainers in the hallway and led me down a corridor into the room where the Asian gentleman had been sitting that morning. A fire was burning to death in the grate and when she left me I stood by it to warm myself while I waited for Emma.

On the mantelpiece I spied a wedding invitation with italicized script on thick white mounting board. Both bride and groom had double-barrelled names, so perhaps the happy couple went for the full Gatling gun on their special day. The room oozed a kind of decayed grandeur and I picked up an old copy of *Country Life* from a strange piece of furniture, a kind of backless sofa or upholstered coffee table. Trembling from shock, I sat on it to flick through the magazine in the hope that I'd look more at ease when Emma showed up. Beneath an oil painting of a pheasant with a long tail some copy settled to read: 'Holland and Holland. In the country, refinement still comes with a double-barrelled name.'

I needed to find somewhere to hide the dictaphone, but I felt dizzy when I stood up and tripped on a frayed patch in the carpet. It made me think of the hessian backing of Jeff's wine-stained rug. And of Mark's pink plaster. Silver-framed photographs covered the top of a Bechstein model-D piano and I felt a host of tiny 2D eyes track me as I weaved my way across the room. I was in no shape to fence Emma into a confession. My mind was moving in the slow way the leaves of house plants turn to the light. Where was she? What if I'd got it all wrong? There were so many photographs of the Bowrings with their various friends and acquaintances that it looked as if they needed to be reminded who they were. I knew the feeling. In one of the photographs Richard had been captured with an expression of panic at a bow-tie gala shaking hands with Prince Charles. Emma stood to one side, sparkling with red-carpet fever. Charles was giving Richard his trademark rictus, as if an angler had inadvertently hooked the side of his mouth and given it a sharp tug. The same love-starved smile was fading to nothingness on my improvised sling.

I replaced the photograph as Emma entered the room with a scarf round her neck. She came forward in a rush, but stopped at the sight of the mud and the blood on my clothes. The past two days had drawn her flesh closer to the bone and her sunbedded skin was pulled tent-tight over the arc of her nose.

'Andy, are you hurt? I saw your van! Are you all right?'

I told her I'd never been better and switched on the dictaphone in my pocket, kicking myself for not having taken the opportunity to hide it behind one of the photographs while I had the chance. I doubted that the microphone would record through the sheepskin even if I thumbed the pocket wide open.

'Did you hit Rolf?' she asked. 'I found him limping on the drive.'

I nodded. Emma was distraught, but it wasn't down to the dog.

'What on earth brought you all the way out here?' she asked. 'I left your money with Ildikó.'

She was trying to be light and flirtatious, but she sounded fretful and a little snappy.

'I came with Phil,' I said.

Her face opened like an ugly flower.

'Oh, Andy, I'm sorry. I didn't know how much he'd told you!'

She leaned against me, as yielding as a stalagmite.

'I can help you,' I said. 'But you've got to tell me what really happened at Jeff's.'

'Jeff's? Jeff who?'

'The flat in Kilburn. I saw you drive away from there the other night in Richard's car.'

She backed off and fiddled with her hair. It was intended to make her look vulnerable and innocent, but it only annoyed me.

'Why didn't you say so yesterday?' she asked.

'Why didn't *you*? Look, I can call the police right now if

you'd prefer,' I said. 'Just tell me what happened!'

Her eyes shifted from side to side like abacus beads as she tried to work out what to say. Red lipstick extended a few millimetres on to her face where a dark pencil line circumscribed the cosmetic's territorial gain. It made her look a tad insane.

'Didn't Phil tell you?' she asked.

'Tell me again. Why did you go round there?'

'I thought Phil was trying to wreck my marriage with those calls. He'd become obsessed. I went to tell him I couldn't see him any more. I'd no idea that Mark would be there . . . Well, as you know, it was a stupid accident.'

She turned to the window and took a deep breath. I took the dictaphone from my pocket and felt its soft hum in my fingers as I placed it in amongst the photographs on the piano. Emma turned back to me, wiping away a crocodile tear before it had a chance to go creeping down the powder-parched delta of her cheek. My heart was racing. I really thought she was about to confess to Mark's murder and I prayed that she'd stay within range of the mike.

'I'd no idea Phil and Mark even knew each other till yesterday,' she said. 'But the moment I walked into the flat Mark realized I'd been seeing Phil. Mark was drunk, really trashed. Then Phil came back without the stamps and Mark went berserk. He said Phil had betrayed him and he punched him and kicked him. That's when Phil hit him with the bottle. It was awful.'

I could just about see Phil doing it, doubling back to the flat after I'd found the body. The thought gave me a cold oily feeling on the back of my neck.

'He didn't know that Mark had a paper-thin skull,' she added. 'It's a medical condition. He'd had it all his life.'

The police claimed Blair Peach suffered from the same

thing when he met the Met and they clubbed him to death. Linton Kwesi Johnson even did a song about it. Certainties were collapsing like poorly assembled flat-pack furniture and I was terrified I'd got everything wrong. In the circumstances, all I could do was to pretend to play along with Emma.

'Jesus!' I said. 'I'd no idea.'

'Phil didn't tell you?' she sobbed.

'No,' I said. 'I don't know what to say. You poor thing.'

Her small eyes brightened a few watts when she thought I'd bought her story. Those eyes were the shop-windows to what was left of her soul and I knew from their sick glow that she'd told me lies; that she was a scheming, amoral bitch who felt no remorse for what she'd done. Now she was trying to shift the blame on to her former lover.

'Where's Mark's body?' she asked. 'Have you buried it?'

'No. It's in a garage near here,' I said.

'But I thought –'

Emma stopped herself just in time. She looked truly scared for the first time, the whites of her eyes visible all the way round the irises.

'I don't understand why you didn't just go to the police,' I said.

'I wanted to, but Phil said it would be better if he handled it.'

I sensed her mind speeding.

'Even though it was self-defence, Phil thought he'd go to prison,' she said. 'And of course I was worried about what it would do to Richard if he knew I'd been there. Then Phil phoned me the next day and said the two of you were going to take the body out into the country. I thought you were going to bury it.'

She dabbed at her smudged mascara with the corner of a handkerchief that she'd pulled from the sleeve of her cardigan. Emma used a lot of eyeliner at the outer edges of her eyes to make them look bigger, but she was a talentless illusionist.

'Phil mentioned that you thought you'd seen Richard at the flat,' she added. 'I suppose that's what gave him the idea of pinning it all on my husband.'

'This is dreadful!' I said. 'You've been through hell.'

She melted into me, convinced that I believed her. She felt nothing for other people. She thought we were all pretending just like her and I dug my nails into my palms to stop myself shoving her across the room.

'Kiss me,' she said.

She pressed against me and pushed her dry little tongue into my mouth. I mashed her lips with mine and my stubble sandpapered her face. I was sick of her and sick of myself.

'Easy, soldier,' she chuckled.

She used a lipstick and a compact mirror to repaint her mouth, pouting a perfect little red round No Entry sign. Emma Bowring was enjoying herself.

'Look, the truth's going to have to come out,' I said. 'Phil's going to have to take his chances. Is that all right? I mean, are you still in love with him?'

She lit a Silk Cut and smoked it as if it was a race.

'Are you joking? Of course I'm not. He's dead weight.'

'Then why don't we just go to the police?'

'Oh, we can't do that, Andy! They'd turn me into an accessory, wouldn't they?'

She wrinkled her nose at the word 'accessory', as if seeing her pre-tanned flesh transformed into a handbag swinging from a crocodile's wrist.

'I don't know, but I think you'd be out in under three years. If they even convict you. Judges don't like sending rich white women to prison.'

'Listen, why do we have to tell anyone I was even there? You could say you saw Phil do it and that it was self-defence, that Phil was provoked. I could make it worth your while.'

Emma smiled with flirtation's last gasp, but she had given me the worst thirty-six hours of my life and I was determined to shake a full confession out of her. When you find out that you've been living a lie, you develop a taste for truth. I just hoped that the tape hadn't run out.

'So that's all settled, but what's in it for me?' I asked.

'What do you mean?'

'Well, you and Richard get a whole heap of money, but what do I get? Just a nasty little slide show for when I can't get to sleep at night. Call it fifty grand. Cash.'

'You're asking me to pay you? Are you crazy? Why should I give you anything?'

'To say Phil killed Mark and that you didn't. Look, I saw Phil find the body, the shock it gave him. You can't fake that. You killed Mark yourself. We both know it, so let's make a deal.'

'That's outrageous!' she shrieked. 'Anyway, you moved the body, so you can hardly go to the police. Mark was a lost soul. Perhaps you are too. Just a sad little loser. You don't deserve a thing.'

'Whereas you deserve to have it all?'

'Yes, absolutely,' she said. 'Except for the job and the kids.'

Phil was standing just inside the door with his face covered in dried blood. I'd no idea how long he'd been there.

'Hi, Phil,' I said.

That got her attention. Emma spun round and saw him.

'Oh, darling!' she cried. 'Thank God you're here!'

She ran to him and he back-handed her across the face, bloodying her lip.

'You fucking bitch!' Phil shouted. 'Trying to stitch me up! I fucking heard you!'

She dabbed at her mouth with her handkerchief.

'I only said it so he'd bury the body! Don't you see? If Andy thinks you did it, he'll help us.'

'Liar! You're just trying to protect your fucking scumbag husband!'

They were staring at each other, their faces shot through with an anger that quickly turned into lust. It dawned on me that the whole thing had been some kind of sick sex-game between them.

'Anyway, it's too late,' Phil said. 'I called the police. Richard's cracked. They'll get him to admit he did it.'

'Oh, you bloody little fool!' she cried. 'You said you'd bury the body!'

'You said you loved me!' Phil spat. 'I only said I'd do that if it meant not going to jail for your fucking husband!'

He slumped down in a wing-back chair and ran his hand through his hair. It was hard to believe that his face had once been the template for a weenybopper crush. Emma knelt beside him and took his hand. There was an enormous mirror on the far wall and they used it to see how they looked. Emma fingered her bust lip with an almost erotic fascination.

'You two were made for each other,' I said. 'A couple of thrill-seeking narcissists.'

Naturally enough, they didn't hear me.

'We had a chance for something and you just threw it away,' Phil said to her. 'No one'll ever love you the way I do, but oh no, you had to go and trade in what looks you had left for a bunch of fucking credit cards. Well, now you get nothing.'

'Are the police really coming?' she asked.

Phil nodded. Emma choked back a sob, but the tears were for herself and her predicament, not for Mark. She was terrified about what was going to happen to her. Phil kissed her and then he tried to smile. It only worked on one side of his face and I thought of Prince Charles and the dictaphone on the piano.

'They'll be here any minute,' Phil said. 'Maybe we can work something out, but you've got to tell me the truth.'

'God, you always see right through me,' she sighed.

Yes, I thought. Because there's so little there.

'Go on,' said Phil.

'Well, I went round to the flat to find you and I found Mark instead,' she said. 'I don't know how, but the moment he saw me he knew. He said he'd tell his father about us. To hurt him. He was so pleased about it all, it was horrible.'

She was speaking in a little girl's voice and the sound of it made my skin crawl.

'I suppose I shouted at him and he attacked me. He pushed me on the floor and undid his fly. He was going to rape me. Actually he started, so I picked up the nearest thing to hand. I never planned it . . . You've got to help me, darling. If we don't bury him, they'll put me in prison. You and Andy too, probably. I mean, you did move the body. We could go away together. Brazil maybe. I've got some money. You could find work.'

'Yeah? Forget it,' Phil said.

He couldn't see himself doing a fifteen-hour shift in a São Paulo sweatshop sewing on swoosh ticks any more than I could.

'Or we could say Andy killed him,' she whispered. 'It'd be two against one.'

'Charming,' I said. 'But you can stop now. I think we've got enough.'

I reached for the dictaphone. When Emma saw the winking red light there was a look of terrible disappointment on her face, as if her world was a peach and she'd turned it round to find it caved in and grey with decay. She made a half-hearted lunge for the dictaphone, but Phil held her back and her scarf came loose. There were deep scratches on her neck.

Ten minutes later the police arrived.

21

Phil and I were taken to a hospital in Swindon, where the doctors shone a light in my eyes, X-rayed my head and put my shoulder back in its socket. Then a consultant told me that my skull was fractured. For the next two days I floated on a marshmallow cloud of medication, telling myself I was lucky and waiting for my teeth to renew their lease on my gums sufficiently for me to chew solid food again. Every so often a nurse came and checked my pupil reaction, pulse and blood pressure. In answer to my questions, she told me that she'd heard Emma was still under arrest and that Phil had been discharged from the hospital into police custody. Richard had suffered a heart attack and was recovering across the Grand Canyon of the social divide in the private wing of the same hospital. The police wanted to talk to me and I wasn't allowed any visitors, but I was thrilled when Sara sneaked on to the ward to see me. She kissed me hello on the lips but she looked exhausted, her mind elsewhere.

'I didn't think you'd come,' I said. 'I thought you'd be too angry.'

'It's not about you,' she said. 'It's Mark. We grew up together. I miss him, that's all.'

I wanted to console her but my tongue flapped about like a fish on a hot metal deck.

'I am angry with you, though,' she said. 'You're such an

idiot. Why on earth didn't you tell me?'

'I didn't want to get you involved.'

'Involved? You left Mark's body in Mum's garage! I even slept with you while he was out there! How do you think that makes me feel? And I've spent the last two days in a bloody police station!'

Her words sliced into me.

'I didn't want to screw everything up for us. And that's exactly what I've gone and done,' I said.

'Oh, for God's sake! Don't look so sorry for yourself.'

'But it's over, isn't it?'

She turned away, preferring to look out of the window at a light industrial estate rather than meet my gaze.

'Who knows?' she said. 'You were brave going up to the house on your own.'

'I'm so sorry,' I said.

There was a strange lag before she replied, like on the transatlantic calls I'd made to Janet in another lifetime.

'You're always saying that,' she said.

I took Sara's hand, but she could muster no more than a thin smile and a perfunctory squeeze in return. When a nurse came on to the ward and shooed her away, I was hoping that she'd turn and wave or even blow a kiss from the door, but she didn't even look back and I had an awful feeling that this time I'd lost her for good. If so, there was no one to blame but myself and the world seemed a bleak and empty place.

Two more days passed before I was taken to the police station and questioned by a detective with a receding chin. As I told him what had happened, I realized just how plain stupid Phil and I had been. No-chin asked me a hundred questions, recording it all on some manky equipment that looked as if it might have been stolen from

Sara's stepdad's barn, but he didn't ask me if I went back to WH Smith for the stamps and I could find no good reason to tell him. After lunch I saw Emma being led past in the corridor with a spring in her step and a bounce in her blow-dried hair. I was scared she'd somehow pin Mark's death on Phil or me yet, even though I knew the police had her taped confession. After the interrogation I was put in a cell, a minimal oatmeal box ten feet square with two wooden platforms covered with thin foam mattresses. Various detainees shared the cell with me over the next six hours, but I discovered little about them. Given the explosive mixture of alcohol, anxiety and criminality, the cell demanded a level of circumspection you'd expect to find in the Vatican or an STD clinic. The police released me around ten o'clock that night, but they were far from happy about letting me go.

'You'd've saved us all a lot of trouble if you'd reported this at the time, wouldn't you?' said No-chin.

Feeling dangerously good, I took a train back to London and, unable to face Jeff's flat, caught a tube to Kilburn and then a bus to crawl up Shoot-up Hill. I jumped off on the corner of Walm Lane in Dollis Hill and crossed the lawns of the Windmill Court Estate, moving through drizzle and pools of sodium light beneath the high-rise that soared vast and insubstantial against the night sky. Facing the estate, the brick terraced houses on Walm Lane had been carved into flats by the developers and dotted with satellite dishes like drawing pins left in a school notice-board at the end of term. I reached my own block, climbed the stairs to the fifth floor and walked down the corridor, inhaling the school smell of disinfected linoleum.

Flat 26 was a small one-bedroom dwelling unit that had

been my home for nearly two years, self-catering years, and as I shut the door a grey wave of loneliness ran over me. There was no message from Sara on the answering machine, just one from the garage that had towed my van from Foxton Hall. A heap of ancient washing-up stood piled in the sink, the very antithesis of interior decoration. If only there'd been a trace of Sara – one cup, one plate – I could have brought myself to attack it. As it was, I kicked off my trainers and tried to call her, but her answering machine was on and I didn't leave a message, anxious that the tape would register my growing despair. Sara seemed a million miles away and Phil's number was still disconnected, so I couldn't even vent my spleen on him. I began to introspect obsessively in my isolation suite and telephoned Sara repeatedly just to hear her recorded voice. I finally cracked on day two, leaving a message that I hoped was sufficiently Up and Light. Over the next few days I added a string of increasingly deranged messages, but she didn't call back and the flat felt smaller and emptier hour by hour.

The police charged Emma with manslaughter and the story broke on a regional news programme with some hastily assembled footage of the Bowrings' house and a clip of Emma acting her little socks off. She'd had a crawl-on part in a Jean-Claude Van Damme vehicle, an experience disturbing enough to have twisted the most well-adjusted psyche into blue touchpaper.

Phil finally mustered the courage to call me and he sounded so contrite that I couldn't be bothered to slag him off for more than ten minutes. Besides, Phil had always been a manipulative tosser underneath it all, and I'd been a fool for thinking that he might have changed his spots. What chance for Germolene against the enduring acne of a thirty-sixteen-year-old? And at the back of my mind I knew that if Phil had lied to me about Emma, I'd lied to him about the stamps. When I asked him about her, there was a catch in his throat as he told me that she'd confessed to manslaughter in the presence of her lawyer. The inquest had revealed traces of her skin under Mark's nails (along with half a gram of silver scratchcard plastic), so there was little she could do but suffer a nervous breakdown. Emma had been released on bail and was recovering in a private clinic under the care of Dr Leffler, Mark's old shrink. I sensed the weasel cunning of an expensive lawyer and began to think she might even get off the manslaughter charge.

'The weird thing is that despite all this I still love her. I really do,' Phil whined. 'There's a real chemistry between us.'

'Sure. Like Bhopal. Or Chernobyl,' I said.

I imagined them living off each other in the moral white-out of Los Angeles, no life outside themselves, their dreams going straight to video and the half-price bin in Tower Records.

'You don't understand,' Phil said. 'The force of it.'

'Of course I do,' I said. 'It's the first time you've ever been chucked, you egotistical git. And you couldn't handle it.'

'Oh really? By the way, I saw Sara the other day,' he said. 'At Dean's.'

My heart thumped its way up my throat.

'Yeah?'

'She's pretty down about all this. You should give her a call.'

'I've been trying her for the past two weeks.'

'She's staying at her mum's flat in Greenwich, but she'll

be at the funeral,' he said. 'I'm going along myself, pay my respects and everything. You should come too. We've nothing to be ashamed of.'

I wasn't sure about that. I'd tried to write Richard a letter, but I couldn't find the right blend of apology and condolence. Still, I agreed to go to the funeral with Phil because it might be my only chance to talk to Sara. He told me that it was to be held at Golders Green Crematorium and I spent the next week in the flat, flat and sad, unable to work because of my shoulder. I'd have signed on if I hadn't already been doing so. As soon as I felt up to it, I went down to the garage in Pewsey. The man said the van was worth a hundred in cash even as it was, so I borrowed a friend's car, signed over the van and retrieved the stamp album from beneath the seat. Determined to return it to Richard Bowring at the funeral, I used some of the money to buy a black suit for the occasion, an Italian double-breasted thing from Oxfam. When Phil came over to collect me on the day of the funeral, he said it gave me all the charisma of a failed digital-TV salesman. As a 'mark of respect' for the deceased, Phil had turned his black Cypress Hill T-shirt inside out. There was something bothering me and on the tube to Golders Green I asked him how he'd met Mark.

'Sara brought him round to Dean's one night,' he said. 'Mark recognized me and he had some nice things to say about the band.'

'That should have set some alarm bells ringing,' I said.

'Hey, come on. Mark was cool enough. I played him some stuff and he wanted to finance the demo. I only found out he was Emma's stepson after you started working there. You know, I really thought it was like a stroke of luck. Can you believe it?'

Then Phil told me again that he'd been working on some songs, a really stripped-down sound – very, very exciting, just an acoustic guitar, much more real than anything he'd done before – and I listened to his spiel as a tragic strip of Northern Line tunnel unreeled behind the train's dark picture windows.

22

We arrived early at the red-brick crematorium and the sun gave off no heat, so I shivered in my new-to-me suit. No announcement had been made in the papers, but a press photographer was already staked out beyond the railings and I imagined a fifty-quid bung for an apprentice undertaker from an uncle on a tabloid. The shutterbug recognized Phil, who duly obliged him with a series of pensive poses, and I half suspected Phil of making the tip-off himself. It turned out that I was dead right, but the case was *sub judice*, so at least the world would be spared Phil's own exclusive story for a few months – the sickening, self-serving pack of lies that provoked me to write my own account.

The hearse arrived, followed by four black funeral cars. Richard Bowring climbed out of the first car with a walking stick, moving slowly as though negotiating a bog in unsuitable shoes, and looking ten years older. The stamp album was in my rucksack and I planned to return it to him after the service. Ildikó was in the second car, pale and drained as if she'd been giving board and lodging to a vampire for the last two weeks. I went over to her.

'I'm really sorry, Ildikó,' I said. 'If only I'd told you –'

'Shh. You're a good boy, Andy. You didn't do this. Not your fault.'

She shook her head and gave me a hug, and I felt partway absolved of the guilt I'd been carrying around. I hadn't realized until then just how heavy it had been. More people arrived on foot and by cab, but I couldn't see Sara. When the funeral director ushered us all into the small chapel, Phil and I hung back to wait for her, watching the undertakers pull Mark's coffin out of the hearse by handles that looked too shiny to be real metal. They slid the coffin on to a steel trolley and wheeled it into the chapel, but there was still no sign of Sara. We followed the undertakers inside as they rolled the coffin directly on to the plinth.

'Nice touch,' Phil whispered. 'They've got it down cold, yeah?'

Had they thought to remove the plaster from Mark's finger? I could still see its pink weave in my mind's eye. Phil pointed out Dean, who was sitting alone five rows in front of us, dark glasses perched on top of his moulting bonce. The cleric made some introductory remarks and then he announced that he was going to play a tape of a song Mark had written. My toes curled and Phil shifted uncomfortably as the first few bars filled the chapel.

'What's going on? This is the tune you played me the other day,' I whispered. 'In the van. You fucking said you'd written it yourself!'

It was a good tune and I felt stab of sadness for Mark. When the song ended, one of Mark's old school friends tried to make sense of his life and as he battled on there was a draught behind us. I fought the impulse to turn round and then Sara passed by and sidestepped into a pew further up the aisle. I felt weightless. We were breathing the same air. Everything was going to be all right.

The coffin wasn't rolled out through the chain-metal curtains. It stayed where it was and we filed past it out into some cloisters that looked on to the garden of remembrance. Dean was shedding drippers from a seemingly limitless reservoir of sentimentality. Mourners mingled, their faces melted by their proximity to the incinerator. I looked around for Sara and inadvertently bumped into Richard.

'Thank you for coming,' he said.

I wanted the earth to chew me up. His tanned face had faded and crumpled like an old ten-pound note.

'I'm really sorry,' I said. 'I should have gone straight to the police.'

'You mustn't blame yourself,' he said. 'No one must. It was just a terrible accident.'

Richard's suffering had made him a little more human, but his words were as empty as the Anglican funeral rite. The truth was that he blamed himself so much that his life was beyond repair. I could see it in his eyes.

'I've brought you the stamps,' I said, rooting in my rucksack. 'Here.'

I held out the album. It took him a moment to realize what it was and then he shook his head.

'Keep them,' he said. 'I don't want them.'

He turned his back and walked away from me without another word. I was stunned and searched frantically for Sara. I was beginning to think she'd already left when I saw her talking to Ildikó over by the car park. They'd both been crying and Sara came over to me.

'It's good to see you,' I said. 'I only came because I knew you'd be here.'

'Well, you've seen Richard too, haven't you? And Ildikó. She tells me I should give you another chance.'

'And?'

'And I don't know.'

Sara said she wanted to leave, so I asked her if I could go

with her and to my surprise she agreed. Phil and Dean were deep in conversation, so we said goodbye to them and to Ildikó and walked to the underground station. Sara didn't say much and I knew enough to keep my mouth shut. The train was fairly full, but we found two free seats opposite a couple in their twenties. It took me a minute to realize they were blind and that their own ill-fitting second-hand clothes had been picked for them by others. I showed Sara the stamps, explained why I had them and gave them to her as something to remember Mark by. As the train pulled out of Chalk Farm, the blind woman squeezed the man's thigh and he put a hand on her neck. Then they kissed each other on the mouth for a long time and Sara and I watched them even as we tried to look away. When our train stopped at King's Cross she handed me the stamp album.

'Let's give it to them,' she said.

It felt like the right thing to do, so I put the stamp album in the man's hands and told him it was a gift. There was so little time and everyone on the train thought I was a nutter, but I made him take it and jumped out just before the doors closed to join Sara on the platform. As the train pulled away the couple were smiling and as it left the station I saw the man laugh at something the woman said.